The Birth of the World as We Know It

Other Books by Meredith Steinbach

Novels
Zara
Here Lies the Water

Story Collections
Reliable Light

The Birth of the World as We Know It; or, Teiresias

a novel by

MEREDITH STEINBACH

 TRIQUARTERLY BOOKS
NORTHWESTERN UNIVERSITY PRESS

Evanston, Illinois

TriQuarterly Books
Northwestern University Press
Evanston, Illinois 60208-4210

Copyright © 1983, 1984, 1988, 1993 by Meredith Steinbach. Published 1996 by TriQuarterly Books/Northwestern
University Press. All rights reserved.

Printed in the United States of America

ISBN 0-8101-5060-3

Library of Congress Cataloging-in-Publication Data

Steinbach, Meredith.
    The birth of the world as we know it, or, Teiresias : a
novel / by Meredith Steinbach.
        p. cm.
    ISBN 0-8101-5060-3 (cloth : alk. paper)
    1. Tiresias (Greek mythology)—Fiction. I. Title.
PS3569.T37546B57   1996
813'.54—dc20   96-24128
                                                        CIP

The paper used in this publication meets the minimum
requirements of the American National Standard for Information Sciences—Permanence of Paper for Printed Library
Materials, ANSI Z39.48-1984.

Contents

Acknowledgments

The author wishes to express her gratitude to the Mary Ingraham Bunting Institute of Radcliffe College, Harvard University, for fellowships and support during the preparation of this work. Sincerest thanks also go to the Rhode Island Council on the Arts, the Yaddo Corporation, and the Thomas J. Watson, Jr., Institute for International Studies.

Parts of this novel have been featured in different form in issues of *TriQuarterly*.

This is a work of fiction. No human persons living or dead are represented here.

I offer special gratitude to Reginald Gibbons and Lee Webster for consistent editorial acumen and encouragement, and to the late Stanley Elkin for his helpful, warm, and incisive influence.

Thanks to friends Alison Bundy, Hortense Calisher, Robert Chibka, Martha Collins, Rita Dove, Barbara Grossman, Allan Gurganus, Michael S. Harper, Moira Hirst, Eithne Jordan, Elizabeth Kirk, Blossom S. Kirschenbaum, Dr. King Liu, Mark McMorris, Joanne Meschery, Peter Gale Nelson, Ronn Smith, Mary Swander, and Keith and Rosmarie Waldrop. Professor Emily Vermeule allowed me to absorb what I could of her considerable knowledge and intellectual bearing while I was on fellowship at Harvard. Special thanks to the people who read hundreds of manuscript pages aloud for me during periods of problematic eyesight several years ago.

And many thanks to the four Graces of our village for having made life in France possible and for immeasurably enriching it.

M. S.

For my father, Christopher G. Steinbach,
and
for Zach, my son

I

The Very Dead

....

They say that my father was killed by Athena before my birth, that she drew back her bow and shot at him through the navel with one of her most expert strikes. It is still said that the forces of my father's life in combination with her blow were so great that his entire body spun on the ground, rapidly at first, and then more and more slowly. At last he became only a shadow there in the dirt. From then on, as sunlight fell over the shaft of the arrow and down around his still-turning form, miraculously time itself could be told by anyone, even a child.

This same Athena, my father's slayer, my mother's lover, advised Kadmos to sow the serpent's teeth, and thus from the seedlike teeth and spit of a snake came the grandeur of Thebes. It was Athena who blinded me, Thebans say. Who knows how they came to believe such a thing. Yet my particular heroism lies partially in that same untruth. Even the most distant village peoples, even those along the sea, living in instability on shifting sands, declared that she had not only taken my vision from me but had also given me second sight. Perhaps in a way she did seal my eyes—to my father's life and what it might have meant: his tenderness and fatherly irritation, the things he knew, perhaps his cajoling instruction into the ways of the world. If I had had the sight of him daily and hour to hour, if I had carried the vision of him when he had gone to another room—right there at the back of my eyes—perhaps I would have been freed from a second sight that has left me always alone and never in privacy. In that way I would have lost my gift. All my life I have prayed to the Gods for the benefits of both.

Now that I am in the Underworld, I see again; yet everything around me, this river pounding against its underground shores, the dead wafting here, there, passing words like honeyed pears among strangers at a feast, all is without substance here. Without line or passion or strength. It is always the beginning here, contrary to what we had all imagined. We had imagined that here it all would end.

One by one, the shades lean down to drink black blood. In a sweat of vapors, along the banks they recline until the magical fluid of their former lives has reached their limbs, until it all comes rushing back to them: how it was. I watch Odysseus as he builds up the fire again. With this same fire he set out, most courageous of men, to conjure me, Teiresias the Compass, from the dead. Now, here we sit attesting to his further powers, for beside this bonfire, answer to all my dreams, my dead Emporous stands in polished brass shield. Emporous the potter is still—in the way of the dead—lovely, dark, mature; pale muscles fill out his upper arms. He looks at me in astonishment. I am an ancient creature, fallen against him in a heap: "What happened to you? I imagined everything: you sold as a slave, driven and tortured. I knew you would have returned—if you could."

All my life and afterward I have heard the inner echoes of my own voice mouthing these words. Now they meet with chilled air, but I cannot stop shouting my lifelong imagined speech: "I stood on our road. When I blinked, a terrible mist had taken your place. My eyes sting for you. Even now. See how they sting?"

"Teiresias?" Emporous asks, incredulous, a shock of hair fallen over his brow. "Are you what's become of my Teiresias?" We stare, each in our turn, into the solid pink and brimming eyes of another one dead.

Off to one side, Odysseus towers, resolute. He cannot take his gaze from us, from Emporous's shield, whereupon lives the bronze head of Kadmos, ancient sign of our lost world, emblazoned there. Of these things, Odysseus has heard. As a boy he bowed down in his playroom to such a shield. Odysseus won't try to leave. He doesn't know his way. Within this nearly hairless, sunken skull, I can see the map to Odysseus's future wanderings. The great warrior shudders at the sight of us. Emporous, whom he has helped to call, is no more than forty-two years old, yet some eighty years in the grave. Nearly two hundred and eight years of life had passed before I was laid in my tomb; beyond that I have been here something like twenty-eight. I can hear what Odysseus is thinking. This is no extraordinary trick on my part; he has always muttered while he thinks.

"Decrepit bodies," Odysseus utters; he believes, privately, "Maybe I am trapped here. I'll be one of them, a grape shriveling." Yet he is amazed. "It's Teiresias," he sighs, "of Thebes, the greatest intelligence ever known. And I am here with him. And there's his boyhood teacher. Who would believe such things?"

Such foolish reverence from heroes without knowledge turns my spittle black. I feel a few words coming on. Even in this deluge of emotion, the prophet speaks. Odysseus cranes his ears, pretending to study the others at the river where they dangle their nearly transparent feet. Over them a clear water drives between rocky banks. I can no longer keep my eye on him. Odysseus is increasingly powerful, a prying and reckless man. "Odysseus," I whisper, and the warrior starts, found out. "Move a little way down the creek, be a good boy." I can see his shoulders tighten as he moves away. A familiar scent is near me, a familiar hand. I can think of nothing else.

I am like a snail now on Emporous's lap. I have curled myself that tightly in his arms. Over there behind that rock, an intruder sits, the one who with Circe's help has made the dead to speak and recall. Odysseus has brought Emporous back. Yet Odysseus's distant schemings make a constant sound: "Not so long ago Achilles was cradled like this," Odysseus, our watchdog, is babbling now. He had not thought history to be so real, the heroes of times past to be so heartrending. He had only thought his own trials to be anything. He sees Emporous, sees his great beauty, sizes up the garb of early metals. "Bronze!" Odysseus is now like a finicky tailor in all things. "And the insubstantial tip of that spear. Look at him! Teacher of the Wise One! Yet profoundly failed as a warrior."

"What is that drivel?" Emporous shouts, gesturing toward Odysseus the Man. Emporous's anger is a thrill running through the scenery. "What is the brightness in that man that drives him so wild? Why won't he give us a moment alone?" Together we stare at him, Odysseus is practically vibrating with color.

How would I explain to Emporous everything that has transpired since his death: the end of Thebes, which had flourished since the beginning of time—the most prominent civilization in the world; the end, too, of Troy; and the part played in that by this windblown man. Our time is too short. I press my thumb to the middle of my forehead and nod knowingly.

"Ah," Emporous says with pity. "The man is mad."

"Emporous, tell me how it was," I, the One Who Knows, must plead again. "I prayed to Athena that she would guide you home. But twice she blinded me, once to my father's life, again to yours."

Odysseus could not look away from the ancient prophet of Thebes and Emporous, that master's former teacher. Here were their ages exchanged and distorted so radically. Even after all that he himself had been through, he found it pitiful, perhaps embarrassing. "Here I am," Odysseus whispered angrily to himself, for there near that field of brambles was a group of his own men, each one of them lost at some time in the last years, hideously, so it seemed to him. "Here I am, gritting my teeth, bound as if to my own ship's mast again. Now, while my living ones wait for me with hunger and anxiety—here I am forced to keep watch over the miserable reunion of the entire boneless populace."

Like moths of reminiscence, here and there, all around him, the dead he had evoked flew out from the mouths of caverns, along yellowed underground meadow and stream, the ground barely touching their feet. The dead, the dead, he thought. I am

4

not one of them. I will not let myself become resigned. I will not grow weary here. For here was something he did not know, and all his life Odysseus had given up everything, honor, love, respect perhaps for the pursuit of it. The unknown. He could not take his eyes away from them. Before him the one he knew even by his stance to be but a temporary warrior, one conscripted to the ranks, that Emporous, teacher of the greatest one, stood up, glared directly at him, and lifted the ancient prophet in his arms. And Odysseus wept as he had not wept. He imagined himself: home again, his own arms bearing his father, his son, his wife.

Emporous ran his hands over the wrinkled face of Teiresias, looking hard, searching for what he had known. "When I left, you had the darkest eyes and in them I knew my life. When I left you, the Gods had done the impossible. You, once a boy, were to hold a baby at your breast. Now you are so old I don't know what I see, whether old woman or man—yet it makes little difference."

Teiresias turned over his hand and slid the backs of his fingernails, coolest pads of stone, over the sides of Emporous's face.

"Now, now," Emporous said, patting him. "I could never stand to hear that weeping in your voice. Stop weeping now. How can you hear if you sob so violently? I am giving your story to you. Here it is: the insignificant story of how fate made me a traitor to you."

It had been recited often in Odysseus's childhood, how the troops marched out of Thebes and met their fate. He had often worried that someday the Gods might turn so radically on him. Often he had said it to himself: at least it is not so bad as that. Yet it was a minor loss for Thebes, the loss of that entire platoon and of the young Polydoros, King Kadmos's son. All his life Odysseus had said to himself: *I am terrified of being underground.* And here he was. Odysseus could not close his mouth while the warrior told of what Odysseus knew to be the end of that particular well-known war.

Emporous placed one arm around the shoulders of Teiresias.

They were seated in the sand, both their backs, young and old, against one tree. "When I went away I took great comfort, beforehand, in thinking that whatever happened to me you would have foreseen it anyway. But now I am very sorry for you." Hesitantly, Emporous kissed the place where Teiresias's brow had made itself a kind of smaller hood of skin at the temple for one eye. "The first year away from you, I was surrounded by the battle cries of the fortified, of those dying but in love. I nearly died of grief because I missed you so. For the most part I was alone. Late in the second year my mortal lot sought me out.

"It was autumn, and already we could not ward off violent and audible shivering, both day and night. We were cloistered along a white beach in the blue and white striped tents you helped to make. I can no longer recall exactly where we were. It was so familiar to me; and yet, now it is gone. How have I forgotten the place of my own death?"

Already the effect of life's syrup on Emporous slipped quietly away. "How did it happen? Please say how it was," Teiresias prodded him.

"The moon had been painted above, beautiful and golden, as if Gephura had secured it there herself, stroke by stroke on the temple wall. How triumphant its radiance, we all noted it. It inspired our confidence that night, and our singing, too. Even I sang with my croakers' voice."

"Your voice?" Teiresias asked. Each feature of his mentor and lover he went over and over again, memorizing them. How soon would Emporous, too, be gone? And for how long? He would never see Emporous again. Most likely he never would.

"You don't remember that, I suppose," Emporous said quite blithely. "Frog throat, you called it. You were such an impetuous boy when I met you. In the middle of my chant, you were sure to screech out in that breaking, half-man voice of yours, 'The croakers' voice is exuberant! Enough, Emporous, with sounding like a snake had swallowed you! Give us a chorus, Emporous!' So you said. You don't remember it? I suppose not, no." He went on.

"I was away, distinctly at war, the tents were set up on the beach, and there was a moon like none of us had ever seen. I sat by Polydoros; he was already king—or had Kadmos already come home?—Polydoros was by his title forcibly entitled to be alone. We leaned together and thought our own thoughts. I had not seen him since we left home, and it was some relief to be with a friend, I can tell you that.

"We had just lifted up our voices when there was the unmistakable sound of rushing sand. It was as if we were all gathered around and listening into the center of a shell. Then the earth began to rumble. I have never heard such a grating sound. Fine cracks, like those along the surface of an egg, began to appear near where we sat, and even under us. One ran directly under my feet. And as I looked down at it, the world began to shake, to open and close, and then to pitch up giant slabs of rock. I was one moment on solid ground, running as you can imagine, beneath some trees; in the next a piercing pain took my leg. And then I could see nothing. I had been swallowed alive. And, well—the rest, the journey here, you have experienced yourself, since you are here."

"Emporous! I, too, lost my sight, but I wasn't crushed! I can hardly bear to think of you crushed like that."

Emporous pressed Teiresias's shoulder, stroked his small round head; and the Old One put his frail fingers to Emporous's chin and burst into tears again.

"How is it, little grandfather, that you can still tremble and weep at the thought? Though you are still my poor young friend, my boy, lover, girl, partner and wife, now time is gone for us. Don't you feel a lessening of emotion after all? I see you and a fondness comes to me, but no, I can't say I dwell in the sorrow. Who can carry memories so close as to remember each pang after these hundreds of years? I don't mean to hurt you by saying it, but only to inquire, that is all. You still feel . . . everything?"

Teiresias pulled back, tucked both fragile elbows tightly into his robe, as if that could take away the sting, and lowered his

head. Such hurt he had not anticipated at this juncture. Somehow one should be beyond the hurtful calamities!

"Ah, but of course you feel it still! There is no seeing the
future without feeling the past, is that still it, my little dear?"
The potter reached out to touch the hunched figure again, but
again Teiresias shrank back. The brown hood had fallen over his
face, yet out from beneath it came the heartbroken voice:

"You remember nothing then? Almost nothing of me, of
what we meant, of simple things like bread together and love?"

"Yes, yes, I remember it now; but for some reason I have not
thought of it—for how long? Perhaps since I first came here.
Perhaps I have thought of nothing at all while I have been residing here. Perhaps it's so. I haven't taken the time to think about
such thoughts."

"What is it you think about then, Emporous? Here you all
are—drifting about me, impenetrable. What mournful dead
you are."

"The contrary, little flower. Think what it is to drift emo-
tionless, stirred to exhilarating freedom by the sight of light
swaying in new-leafed trees. That is what it is to be one of us.
You have felt such things. Old One, I pity you, my old friend,
to have no peace even now. You pity us, and we do not even
recognize your pain. What anguish you drum up by calling me,
and what joy; yet it's as if I had returned to a nightmare already
a hundred times borne, and at the end its sweating silent scream
must still be endured. Why do you call me? Why do you put
this on me after all this time? What can be the good of it? For
the momentary thrill of recognition—of ourselves as we once
were, of ourselves as we still must be. That doesn't change.
You're still the little boy I knew so long ago. Your impetuosity
drives you mad, and your gift drives you sane. The first makes
you happy, the last constantly saddens you to the frame."

And Emporous held up his hand, "But, you wish to know.
You wish, as always, for every detail of how it came to be. It was
not a terrible death. I suppose I received a crushing blow. I was
snuffed out easily. Earlier that day I had been thinking constant-

ly of you, but that was nothing new. Every day it was the same. The other men were with their boys, I conjured you. The other men spoke of their wives and children, I conjured you.

"When others were left alone, their lovers killed, still they did not take me on as one of them. I had loved the magical one who had been both boy and woman. I was alive among uncaring idiots, and you seemed dead and gone. Then it seemed an eternity. I mourned.

"As for telling you, I would have, of course. I controlled as little in my life as any man. What could I do to relieve your long-lived anxiety and grief? Could I have sent you word by way of thought? I tried it a hundred times. I was only slightly more efficient than the next spear-bearer in the troop. My weary one—is it really you? Yes, I was killed and buried in the same stroke—it was the earth itself that finished me, and us."

"To be swallowed whole!" the ancient wise man said. "You as nothing but a lump of bread in the throat of some avenging God! What horrific game was that? And by yourself!"

"The detail is no more significant than the whole in cases such as this. You know very well that there is no other way to die than alone, though I admit it: the imprint of a hand on the glove of your bones might linger a moment, might have for a moment been a glad thing."

The round figure rocked forward where he crouched to look up at the yet-handsome man's face. "I never thought I'd see you, of all people, Emporous, grown jaded by death. You've lost all sense of happiness."

"Perhaps," Emporous said, stroking back the white silken hairs around Teiresias's face and taking the trembling paws of the old man in his own. "Or the sense of grief. In any case, I will give you what you want. Isn't that the way it has always been—with us, I mean. There isn't much to hear." Emporous sighed, rested his feet on the upturned shield, and went on:

"With the sudden upheaval of the ground, the waves, too, churned up in a terrifying irregularity. It seemed as if the waves had corners and height beyond imagining. They stood above us like battlements and then fell down. The last I heard was a giant hushing noise, and then I encountered a monstrous constriction in my chest. I could not move my mouth. The chin strap had been applied before I ceased to breathe. I, the potter, was encased not in water but in ground." Emporous laughed, "The potter's funeral urn turned out to be the earth itself! Always the corkscrew of predicament, isn't that the way of our countrymen? Isn't that the way Thebes must be to this very day?"

No smile came onto Teiresias's lips at the mention of the ruined town. "We, too, had that quake," he said. "The central walls fell down. I wept uncontrollably. I didn't know why."

"Ah, for the loss of me you cried and cried. If it had been the reverse I would have done the same. But tell me, you must have known, what of our friend Polydoros? I was with him for a time, as he was the only one who would come near me. I lost track of him the same moment I lost track of everything."

"I thought perhaps you might have fallen in love with him— at times I hoped it was true."

"I spoke with him. We had a song, as I've told you, on the night I've just described."

"If only I had foreseen just one thing truly important in my life! My ill fate follows me everywhere."

"You are modest in that, too, even to this day. You were the one who told me we would not go to war together, weren't you now? But what of Polydoros? Did he come home to Antiope?"

"He did and he did not. His broken body was already here when he came home to the truth of Antiope. He didn't have to hear how she had borne twin sons to Zeus while he was away— while Polydoros's son, the little Labdakos, still nuzzled his baby-boy face at the back of her knees."

A great excitement came over Teiresias's features then. He talked on very rapidly. "There are so many things you will want to know. Things I will be glad to tell. You will want to know about Leiriope, how she built up an island called Gla in the middle of Lake Kopais. All the outer walls of her structure were coated with bronze, just as she had designed, and in them could be seen a river of waves. It was said by everyone who went there that if she walked the beach that ran around the outer city walls, she was just the same blue. It made her entirely invisible—there between ocean and sky. Her plan came true; she made it. Finally she gathered her strength."

Emporous squinted his eyes, already a vagueness in his voice. "Leiriope?"

"Narcissus's mother, surely you remember her."

But Emporous had already begun to turn his head away from Teiresias, who still went eagerly on, spilling out tale after tale of what he knew and remembered still, of how the country people had become so incensed at the beauty of Leiriope's structure that they had torn it down. "Yes!" Teiresias said. "Even in the Underworld you will be surprised to know that in response to their viciousness our Leiriope built a series of viaducts and water tunnels and drained Lake Kopais, the entire thing! Why, your own first wife went there to live with her."

But Emporous's gaze wandered more and more unsteadily. Then suddenly, to the astonishment of the nearly forgotten Odysseus, Old Teiresias was abruptly seated alone on the ground. One moment the two had been coiled together like mother and child, and the next, Teiresias was grieving and Emporous striding away, his shield again on his left arm. "Old man," Emporous called brusquely over his shoulder to Teiresias, as though he'd never met him, "Old man. Do you know this countryside? Can you point me the right way?"

Never before the eyes of the Gods was there a human being so set upon by rumor as Teiresias, never was there a face among men and women so easily inflamed by indignation. Never was anyone so sensitive as this one they called Little Rub Away, Heavenly Body, He Who Delights In Signs, Tender One, Novice. During the long course of his life, false words soared about him. He had been blinded, they said, at the age of seven, having seen Athena in the bath with his mother. Vaguely the townspeople remembered it—the frail and sightless youth with dark hair, groping his way among the trees and along the newly paved road between Thebes and Orchomenos. Nothing could have been more untrue. Far into his fifties, he remained as dark-eyed and unclouded as one of the King of Thebes's most remarked-upon horses. Yet, by the end of his seventeenth year, he was all he would be.

It was true that he enjoyed a sex change for a brief period of his life—seven years, no more, no less. This, too, the natives distorted, bandied about, and spread onto several continents. In the perception of the world, and only there, he fluttered irresolutely between the sexes—first one, now another—until finally as a woman, Teiresias, they said, was changed into a mouse, her lover into a weasel. Is it any wonder then that he/she, when beset by such accusations, turned to birds for insight, for conversation? Such is the fate of prophets, kings, and the immortal mad ones.

II

His Mother's Words

That Europa, Agenor's daughter—skinny and impressionable—had been tantalized by the form the God had taken: the pure white hide of the immense animal, the one black mark of death on his forehead, and the cool pink horns. "Oh, what perfect sport it was when it started," Teiresias's mother told him. "The young woman with the russet hair rushing toward the bull, the one never before among her father's cattle, her father's cattle never before on the beach.

"Up sprang the other girls' warnings
as she plucked the bright blue flowers
from the rocky seascape and flung them at the beast.
Behind her, the companion's cries—like a lyre.

"Closer she skipped as passively the bull rested his eyes on Knossos, on the rising tide of the Mediterranean between Tyre and that island. Her buds pelted the black star, the white nest of fur between his horns; and the bull's mild breath issued from the downy nostrils, moistening the edges of her open bodice and the swellings there. Her little chest was unpainted; she was that young.

"And try, Teiresias. Imagine Europa's surprise: to find the bull so gentle toward her—rubbing its long dewlaps against her shoulder, nuzzling her arms. Then, flaunting her courage before her playmates, Europa mounted the God himself, her skirts hiked up to her thighs, her pink toes spurring his hairy flanks.

"The shore people stand as witnesses—they were the ones

13

who saw it," Teiresias's mother said in answer to her son. Round and round went the brush as Chariklo started at the periphery of one breast, painting toward the center, stopping now and then to change from purple to silver, outlining every segment with a thin black shape. Meticulously she spiraled in on herself until, the young boy saw, she had completed half her morning preparations, she had made a final ring of blue-black specks and at the center one sharp crimson dot. She had chosen the red, she said, because they were going off to meet a friend who had a particular liking for that color, although the friend, a Goddess, was not calm enough herself to wear it.

Lightly she oiled the other breast and dusted it with powder. The little boy watched the camel-hair brush dipping into the palette. The brush had come from Egypt, from Thebes—the other one, Chariklo said, smiling at him with her enormous gray-green eyes in that engaged way that made him think of owls. Teiresias watched her nipple wrinkling like fine cloth, standing out as slowly the brush approached it. "The other Thebes," she blinked. "The one in Egypt." In the window, his back to the courtyard, he felt his little legs swing out, bounce back off the summer currents of the room that meant to him the things he saw, and then he felt the sudden jolt at the heels of his sandals as they struck against the wall beneath him: what he felt. Back and forth he pumped his stumpy legs, hoping she would not again interrupt herself. He waited for the song in his ancestry to rise up, fall again, and soar in the oblivion of his mother's voice.

Europa was on the animal, the boy was in the window, the brush moved back and forth: "'Oh, look out!' the little girls exclaimed as they saw Europa's womanhood approaching vaguely now, for the bull had begun to amble, slowly, toward the water. It was then that the great God Zeus, in bull's attire, walked cheerfully into the sea, swimming with his prize astride his back; and it is said that the sudden moisture of her hot wet tears was no less than that of the ocean his underparts were parting then.

14

"All life's matters are relative things," his mother said, "even for the young and impressionable, and what would seem from afar a terrible or a beautiful fate might have looked quite the opposite to a young girl setting her foot again on solid but confusing ground, or to us thinking of it now in our home, or from the viewpoint of an old man mending nets on the beach. One old man was said to have witnessed it, but all he would say was *a bull, a girl,* and *an eagle on the wing.* Which was wise," his mother said. "It is no small matter to infuriate a God who may at any moment turn himself or a man to a beast.

"It is said that the bull turned his amber eyes halfway around in his head to see the slender girl standing beside him, clinging to his ear. In thought, he pawed the ground beside her scrawny legs, her delicate feet. When Europa looked again, her hand was resting on an eagle's head. Even Gods show a little pity now and then.

"And who is to say how Europa felt? She would never answer questions, and it is not for Gods to speak of their activities to men. Perhaps when he parted her legs with his bitter talons, feathers were lost in the fray; perhaps that day she drew the ichor of a God with her human hand, and rightly so—some say. Maybe the God folded her in the soft down of his new-formed wings as he took her from behind, as birds are wont to do. And then again, perhaps she stroked his golden beak and welcomed him. After all, young women, too, have their own desires. There are many points of view.

"Needless to say, the thing was done.
The penis of a bird entered the body of a woman;
and three sons were born.

"But that is a matter far away from you sitting there in your tunic, with the sun in the window behind your head, from me sitting here each morning painting my breasts, and also from the manner in which this little girl's obsessive brother Kadmos, now our king, determined the fate of Thebes."

From the window he could see a sparrow perched across the way, a sprig of cypress clutched in its beak. Teiresias saw the mottled chest, the dark green twig, the small splayed feet.

"Will you think of it!"

Startled, the bird rose in an arc, turned on the wind, and disappeared. Teiresias, too, twisted at the sound; he felt his own little neck turn halfway around to face the center of the room. "When you set out finally to do something, Teiresias," his mother was saying to him now, the orange-tipped brush pointed his way, "put your goods down in the marketplace. Take your chance. Do not *sway* in the face of distraction. Above all, keep your head!"

But the boy Teiresias had not been at all tempted toward disloyalties, nor had he been tempted by the little bird. She is painting too fast, he thought; she will stop before Father even gets into the story again. And then it was as if he had had two thoughts at once, and nothing was lost for either one in company. The ideas had borne each other up. He set the image of the bird as in a ring around what his mother said. Wing to wing— eagle to sparrow and eagle again—around the picture of what he heard. His mother smiled at him, poured little drops of paint in a vibrant circle around the board she held up in her hand.

"All the sons of Agenor were shipped out of Phoenica—" she said, "the wife and mother, too—in pursuit of Europa, that sparkle turned cinder in her father's eye. Phoinix, Kilix, Phineus, Thasus—each went his own way in search of the red-black hair, the lost child. Kadmos, that eldest brother, wrapped his young arm around his mother's shoulders and together they set the straight horn of his ship into a polished sea. On that ship it was as if their goals were bound together for the first time in their lives; or so the report came back. Telephassa, the anxious mother, said 'Europa' even in her sleep. In a rocking sea, she woke up crying at the thought of a bull dancing on its two hind feet. 'Yes,' her son called from the next compartment. 'There.' Briefly he tossed. 'We will.' But now we know that Kadmos was saying a word that he would not have uttered aloud. To himself he said: *Escape.*

"Now, our king was civilized in his youth. Wherever he went he caused civilization to spring up. It was a storyteller's dream. No, he could not bear the uncultured life, and everywhere set about rectifying the countryside. In Telephassa's grief, she could not understand that just as some cannot bring themselves to speak to the ill or defamed, the romantic Kadmos could not even think of looking at his sister again." His mother stopped.

Again Teiresias looked up to find the source of silence in his mother's voice. Again he felt the two worlds collide: *then* and *now*. "Are you tired?" she asked.

"The cow, the snake, the cow," he cried.

"All right," she said. She reached out as if to pat him across the distance of that room. The hand went up and down on air, and he felt it in his hair. She nodded, and on it went.

"It was in Thrakia that Telephassa took her stand. She looked out over the Edonian's highway where that road wound through open spaces like a peculiar line on a wrinkled face. Out from the Edonian city it went through rocky ground and unadorned hillsides salted with sheep. It stretched like a ribbon all the way up the farthest incline, and there it stopped. Beyond it: there was nothing at all. She saw the warriors clustered together, and her son pointing toward it with a stick, sketching buildings, bridges in the air. It was there in Thrakia that Telephassa—that weary mother of Kadmos, Phineus, Thasus, Phoinix, Kilix, and Europa—raised one finger toward her industrious son and died, to her own relief.

"It cannot be said that Kadmos did not mourn his mother. He could not think of his mother without thinking of his sister; he could not think of Europa without thinking unthinkable thoughts. Carried away by a bull. He had not seen it himself, but he had been told. It was then Kadmos's guilt took on the most simple shape. He would take his men and follow a *cow* until he found his sister and set his mother's dust to rest. Around the country he followed the confused animal, giving way to his old obsessions at every turn. He laid down the foundations of the world wherever that cow lifted up its tail. And that is the way of all civilizations," Chariklo said, flinging her dark hair back. "They begin in dung and end in dung, and in between: a great flourishing of growth.

"A vision of home came to him one day as he stepped absentmindedly along the road, giving up his chariot for the sake of exercise. His mind was not for once on his work. One of his men had counted it out for him: it was his birthday—his nineteenth year—and he was thinking of his personal history as all people do when an anniversary comes around. 'Oh!' he cried aloud, for he just then remembered his soft Phoenician bed in which he had lain as a boy, staring at the cracks that even there traversed the ceiling like glorious viaducts. He had seen the ceramic pots lined up like vats on his windowsill and his private bath with its imperturbable new plumbing. He had seen his mother's own plump maids grown now into eagerness for his engineering ways.

"On he strolled, dreaming of his own place in the world, to which he could not return, following almost automatically the receding haunches of the cow, which had led him through brambles and thickets, over beds of shale. Now suddenly the distant orange flanks loomed large. For this, Kadmos needed no oracle. He had placed his sandaled foot smack in the middle of the modern world: something steaming, something ghastly, large and warm.

"At his shout, throughout the skeletal town, something stirred again in his men that had not budged for years. They threw down their tools and thought the thoughts of warriors; they catapulted to his side. Here they found our king leaping up and down, shouting into the wind at a small orange speck swatting flies on a distant hill. He had stepped, cried out our leader, in the blasted, ultimate, and last site of his building career! Back and forth he paced on that narrow strip of land that is now the street in front of our own house, dragging one foot deliberately through the weeds and calling for the cow and a battle-ax.

"When his warriors had returned with them, Kadmos set forth his first decree. Musical instruments, he declared, would be strung around each bovine neck. Vaguely his men smiled as they sat at his feet. They scratched their heads, imagining it. They looked a long while into their brass armbands. Henceforth, *bells*—he clarified—would serve as a warning to all who came after cows in years to come, on earth or in the Underworld, to keep always the strictest presence of mind. The tinkle would serve as his personal salute to Athena, who knew always where to step and when.

"Bewildered, the men were dismissed to the spring to shovel up water for the sacrifice; and Kadmos was left to curse his authoritarian father, his wayward sister, his domineering mother, his own obsequious life as he tethered a cow: most accursed, brown-eyed, flat-footed thing. He sharpened his ax.

"It was then that he heard the tune rising up, slowly at first, as if it were merely a part of his self-admonishments, a sort of incantation in the background of his immature distress. He lifted up his head. It was as if all his men were singing together and each one without half his tongue. When Kadmos reached the water, he found them in a bunch, as if they had gathered there with the intention to converse. And there, wrapped entirely round and round their collective waist was a highly respectable snake—if size alone is reason for respectability, as is so often said.

"How Kadmos killed the snake is of little consequence, as there are many varying reports and you have heard them all. Some say he poked its eyes out with a branch whittled from the poplar tree; others say he tickled it to death with the pinfeather of the native grouse tied to a long stake. Kadmos's own story as he ages is no less variable than the rest.

"When the snake had died, his men fell apart, one from the other, as petals do when even the smallest flower blooms and wilts and casts out parts of itself finally onto the ground. From this ongoing collapse, those few survivors crawled gasping away to watch in humility their less fortunate companions fall straight over like felled trees. For Kadmos, very little, as we have seen, has ever been enough. Let us say just this—wild-eyed and unpredictable as a sphinx, the young Kadmos sprang upon the viper's corpse, hacking it into unsavory bits, crying out epithets and yanking from its yellow throat a heap of glittering teeth. Upon this pile of carnage that youth—who had, even at nineteen, never known the body of man or woman—the man who is now our king, swore an oath and spat.

> *"From the rock soil and those serpent teeth,*
> *by way of Kadmos's finicky watering—and to his bleak*
> *astonishment—sprang up spears like young asparagus*
> *and with them the forearms of living men, and then*
> *the fully clad bodies of an ancestor*
> *and several relatives of yours. On each man*
> *was the mark that all of us, who have come through*
> *that long line from snake to man, now bear.*
> *No, it was not a blemish: more of a brand,*
> *wine-red and shaped like the head of a spear."*

The young seer looked toward his mother. It made him dizzy to think of it, to look at her. The one breast spiraled one way; the other spun left until the viewer warmed the fingers of his spirit on the bright red centers of those orbs. "And that," she said, "was the beginning of your father's family and yours." She pulled her coat on and motioned toward the door. "There you have it." But what did he have? What was it in the speech of an eagle, he asked himself, that could determine the fate of that willowy young girl, the fate of his own family, of Knossos and Thebes?

They say that when even the smallest fish jumps, a circle is formed and then another, that its leap is felt on every shore. I had never seen such a thing, but they said it was true. My father took me to hunt turtles once. I suppose in a way it was a similar thing. The turtle, my father said, was the most ancient and therefore the wisest of living beings. Even then, starting on the long road to the sea, I thought—there are many ways of looking at the world. We started out from town on foot. I remember my mother leaning out, half-painted in the early morning, from the window. Her eyes were very large.

"It is most important in the hunt," my father said, clearing his throat as he often did when the need for authority hampered his voice, "to adopt the turtle's every thought." I was only seven then, and this was not hard to do. When my father laid his hand on my back, it was as if a golden carapace had settled there.

In my father's lifelong search for wisdom, he rarely allowed his thoughts to interfere with his stride. On this day there was no exception. He possessed two long, thickly muscled legs bronzed by the sun; and on these he moved along so rapidly that every once in a while, to my great embarrassment, he would turn and find me gone. *"Well?"* he asked. His stern blue eyes and long white hair had made him something of a God in our community, and as he stared at me I felt my own lank dark hair growing darker still in his view. As I had no answer to his question, finally the moment passed. I kept up with him for a while until slowly I saw again the one blue vein throbbing at the back of his knee, the broad back, his long purely white hair bounding like a ram between his shoulder blades.

My father must have been deep in thought, and this, I thought, was unfortunate, for I had time to run furiously toward him again and again before I was hopelessly lost, before I saw him, grown small with his traveling, turn suddenly in the road. *"Well?"* he would say when I had caught up with him again. I wished that I had been the pebbles in the road he walked upon.

His eyes are in the sea, the others often said with reverence. You are the son of Sea-Eyes. I had never seen the sea, but I imagined it to be an especially terrifying sight. When I was older I came to think that it was the fear of knowing exactly what they saw in him that made me so slow and disappointing to him that day. On we went, starting and stopping. *"Well?"* he asked, shifting the bag he carried from one shoulder to the other. What kind of bag it was I do not know. It was as if it had not been on his shoulder until we were halfway there. I only remember that it was blue. Or red.

On our journey there was a moment when we stood side by side. This I remember tenderly—perhaps because we were not in motion then. It is hard to follow after a God. The sun was nearly overhead as we stood there gently watering a rock, I remember. And a snake. "Hmmm," my father said, looking down at me in the sort of communion that fathers often feel when standing next to their sons. "I didn't know you had the mark." For there on my penis, at the very tip, was the wine-red mark he bore on his own arm. I think now that he would have been more accurate in his response to our common nature if he had sat down right there in the dirt and wept for me. But he did not. "Hmmm," he said, and rumpled my hair enthusiastically.

We went on again, stammering in our progress. *"Well?"* he asked while I shuffled my feet in a circle in front of him. When I had dragged myself up alongside him for perhaps the twentieth time, he asked it again. This time I did not turn away. My own sullen eyes met his severe ones. My feet grew into the dirt as he shifted the bag from shoulder to shoulder, waiting for my reply. Neither of us looked away. Under his breath he was muttering it again—*"Well?"*

"Well?! Well?! Father, *well* is a hole with water in the bottom of it!" I cried.

My father, the God, rolled his eyes upward toward those of his own kind. In this way he went in search of further wisdom.

I do not remember which had the greater effect on me, the turtle or the sea. I have seen turtles since and always I remember my father then. I have never seen the sea again and I have never been able to forget it. "We will be like turtles," my father said, picking me up and plunging me into the waters. "We will wash ourselves before we come again onto the land." It was true for me then; I could see what the others had said. There, standing up to his brown thighs in what they called the sea, was my father and in his eyes he carried the waves, and at the center of each, a turtle was swimming.

When we were on the sand again, my father opened the bag he had carried such a long way and took out a blanket. It was green; I am certain of that. Bright green. Already he had spotted the tracks of the turtle, but he spread out a blanket and took out his cache of food. He had brought along a sack of figs, of which I had a few. I ate some olives, a piece of honey cake, and drank a little wine. We ate these things then because my father said a turtle in its wisdom would not give itself up to a hungry man.

It was late afternoon, and it was getting a little cooler as we set out after the turtle. We had a piece of rope, a stick, and the blanket. I was given the stick to carry. When we came upon the turtle up the beach a ways, I was disappointed. Oh, it was not the turtle that disappointed me, it was a magnificent turtle. Nearly four feet long with a fine shining shell, and in that shell was the red blood, so my father said, of all the living creatures it had eaten. It was the capturing of the turtle that disappointed me. Yes, it was exciting to hold out the stick and see the monster snap at it, but how quickly and effortlessly my father threw the blanket over its head and wrapped the rope around the cloth-covered neck.

This was the very place where we would lie down to sleep, my father said. We would allow the turtle to collect his thoughts; if we gave him the blanket he would give us our wisdom. During the night I woke shivering with the cold. The sea was pounding against the cliffs down the shore. Here we were without our blanket, and my father stretched full length on the beach, whistling in his sleep as I shivered.

As I nestled under the blanket with the turtle, I thought: it's like lying beside a warm rock that slowly cools as the night goes on. The turtle's head was well covered and I felt no danger. Once during the night I woke to find its claws gently scratching along my arm as if to relieve me of some pain, but in the morning I woke to find myself alone, the edges of the blanket neatly tucked around my feet and shoulders. And there on the beach a fire was glowing, beside it my father was crouched next to the bronze ax. The lovely underbelly of the turtle had been split open, and my father was roasting its heart on the stick.

In the Underworld this life in death is strange as pubescent change. . . . These hands at the ends of my own arms. Whose hands are these shrunken to a lesser glove? Hair gone light and sparse all over the boneless skull. And sprung up like a winter's wheat is moss all over my long-lost chest and chin. This Underworld is worse than anything. It's a crick in the neck!—from all the looking up at that which once required the gazing down.

They will tell you the light in Greece is soft as the thoughts inside a blind man's softly lidded eyes. I myself have seen these lives from many points of view. Life itself is a mosaic on a temple wall only to be constructed, torn down, reexamined, and perhaps rebuilt. My own life was not unusual—to me. Born a male, I bore two daughters in my time as woman; there they are: Manto and Historis, floating now with the rest of them. It was as if each held half of me. Manto in life looked toward the future; in Historis the past was to be found.

For only seven years I had been a woman; it had seemed quite difficult enough. And then, much later, I gained yet another perspective on the world, oddly connected to all that had come first. It came when I was over fifty years of age, not so old and not so young. The girls were already grown, and I was living the third passionate segment of my life. I had for a long time been fitted in the category of man again. No, it was not an unusual day for me when it started out, that day when Hera called me from my contemplations and my earthly activities to decide a dispute for her and Zeus. What I was doing I do not recall. It is insignificant. To say I was not comfortable on the mountaintop would not be to exaggerate. Side by side they sat, the great Gods Zeus and Hera, who was Zeus's wife—and sister, be it known to history.

"You've been both sexes," Hera said, getting directly to the point. Already I was miserable. My greatest trepidations had always been about being asked just this. "Now Teiresias. Who has it better in sex? The man or the woman? Come on," she said. "You can tell us. Who has it the best in sex?"

As soon as she said it, I felt torn apart, as if rent by dogs, not an unfamiliar feeling in my life as seer. But there was a certain finality about this, this simple questioning of mortal by Gods. When had any other mortals been questioned by Gods and not come out the worse for it?

"If you can learn to walk on fire or water," I said, impertinently, "then the rest comes easily."

"Pardon?" she said. "I don't understand."

"I don't know," I said. "It was something from the future. Only time can know what it means."

"Time," she said. "We've seen what your father has made of time."

"Father Time is not a bad name for him," I said defensively. "It certainly has nothing to do with my mother. She's never concerned herself much with him."

"Stop dawdling," Hera said, not unpleasantly. "Give us the answer to the question."

"You could ask Echo," I said. "If you can find her. Perhaps you know where she is. Echo has had a good understanding of others in her life. She may not have felt what it is to be a man, but she has felt the exact repercussions of it."

"I've had enough of Echo's view of things. I'm not looking for reflections. I'm looking for real experience," Hera, the Goddess of marriage and motherhood, said.

"Look at him there," Hera said. "Look at Zeus. He says women have it better in sex—that men merely facilitate it. Facilitate!"

Zeus looked up, his elegant head fringed all the way around in beard and bangs and beard again. His eyes nearly transparent with the golden power in him.

I will not answer this question, I said to myself. These gigantic cats called Gods, I thought, are batting me around. No, I will not answer it.

"Oh come on," Hera said. Her beauty was just as everyone

had ever said. "You know how playful Zeus is. He's prone to change. He's tried everything—almost—at least once."

"Yes," I said. "I've heard such stories. But it's not for a mortal like myself to say whether or not the stories are true."

"Oh come on, Teiresias," Hera said. "Don't play dumb with me. You can see everything, backward and forward, male and female, all of eternity."

"That doesn't mean I can interpret such things," I stammered at her.

Zeus sat back looking bored. "I told you he wouldn't know what to say. Why do you prey on these mortals?" he said. "Why don't you let them go on their way?"

"Why do I prey on mortals?" she scoffed. "You're the one turning into animals of every sort."

"Oh stop," Zeus said. "Just stop. You're boring our guest."

"That's all right," I said hurriedly. "I'll be heading home now. I've been doing a little study of birds myself. It's time I got home to watch their feeding patterns. I see you understand my interest. The observation of their schedule is very acute."

"Now, now," Zeus said, nodding and smiling at me. "Yes, an interesting thing, birds. Yes, you wouldn't believe how glorious it is to take flight and then to settle down on a current of air that takes you directly to the one you love—who may be ascending the air herself. What would you think of that, Teiresias?"

"That is just about enough," Hera said. "You can do what you want when you're alone, but not while I'm around. You don't have to talk about it!"

In the distance then, coming around the corner, was an approaching crowd of Gods. Anyone would have known them. Their size and their posture would have been enough to single each one out, even without their certain telltale radiance: Demeter, Artemis, Aphrodite, Apollo, Hermes, Hephaestus, his face aglow still with his day's work at the forge. Poseidon was dripping wet. Hestia, Asclepious, Prometheus, Atlas, Mnemosyne, Themis, Ares. And there, too, were the Muses, the Hours, the Graces, and the Fates. There also, and particularly foreboding, was Athena herself; they were ambling my way, coming to hear the latest round of argument, curious to see me myself, the weird Teiresias, standing in a veil of sweat, trembling. They were a dangerous crowd, rebels and the descendants of rebels. Not long ago Uranus and Gaea had been in control, soon to be supplanted by Kronos, and then again by Kronos's own son Zeus, and this group. Certainly I was not about to mention these things in front of Hera, who was known for her wrath. They were not my chief interest nor my concern in the world. Yet I was most unfortunately the concern of the Gods at the moment, acutely so.

"All right," Hera said, addressing them. "I've brought up the peculiar Teiresias. Everyone has heard of him. Since he's been both sexes, I thought he could resolve a little dispute Zeus and I have been having. Not that we have many," she said, smiling quite brilliantly.

To which her friends the Gods all groaned.

"Now, now," she said. "Let's see what the One Who Knows says, the One Who Knows What Even the Gods Do Not Know. What will he say? Zeus here has decreed that women have it better in sex. Now we all know Zeus is not a God of little experience in these things. He has been any number of things with any number of women and girls in the realms of sexual pleasure. He's been bull, eagle, horse, and mule. But never a woman or a little girl. There is some justice in the modern world. I see you, Themis, nodding over there. Think of all the children Zeus has fathered in his more sensitive rampages. Why, a few of you are the issue of his philandering."

"Come on," Zeus said. "Get to the point."

"The point is," Hera said, "I say men have it better in sex. And Teiresias is here to say I'm right."

"Well actually—" I said quite carefully. Already I could feel a peculiar burning at the back of my head. "I'm not sure I can actually say anything about it really. You're really talking about male and female Gods, aren't you now? I'm talking mortal sex, not divine sex here. Yes, yes, divine sex would be too big a difference for a mortal to contemplate."

"Ah, but you are the great Teiresias," Hera said. "We aren't talking mere mortal here. Don't be so humble, Teiresias. We know who you are. Give us the benefit of your powers."

"I have decided to tell you how to comfort people," Chariklo said to the very young Teiresias. "First of all, you must be attentive. There is no greater discouragement to one who is already discouraged than for him to tell his woes, after much welling up and fighting of tears, to a mere lump of a face or to one that is always veering toward the window, toward some more interesting project. You must look the victim in the eyes, even if he does not look at you. When he glances up, your eyes must be there on him. The more they are avoided, the more lost, the more victimized. Now here is a young man sitting before you. Can you imagine it? Yes. You are looking into his eyes. He is telling you of the death of his father, or of a serious illness he himself has contracted. Now what do you do?"

Teiresias plumped the pillow he was holding. It was red and gold, a peacock embroidered on it, variegated from eye to tail. "I say I'm sorry, I wish it hadn't happened."

"Look at me when you say it."

Teiresias looked up. He stared into her wide eyes. He could see the young man before him, lost, forlorn, without a father. "I'm so sorry. I wish it hadn't happened to you, to him."

"Now say his name," Chariklo said. She did not take her eyes away.

"But I don't know his name."

"Make one up then."

"I'm so sorry, Terry. I wish it hadn't happened."

"That's much better," Chariklo said. "Do you hear the difference?"

"I do. I think I do, that is. I sort of do."

"If a person feels lost, Teiresias, that person feels nameless. Everything has a name, every kingfisher, cuckoo, pigeon, stone. And in each one a spirit. You say Terry's name, already he feels better. He is really there, he knows it now. And you are there and you are listening. Do you understand?"

"Yes," Teiresias nodded.

"Now go on. What do you say next?"

"I say, tomorrow the sun will shine and we will play ringstick in the yard. You can use my new stick if you want to." Teiresias smiled proudly at himself, at his mother who was named Mother, Chariklo.

"Yes, that's very good," his mother said, leaning forward to pat his knee, to rumple his hair, to squeeze his small arm. "But you don't say that for a while yet. You wait until you've both said other things. Do you know why?"

"He doesn't like to play ringstick, Mother?"

Chariklo threw her head back. She laughed. She squeezed his small, palpable arms.

"Yes, I have powers," I said to Hera, "somewhat extraordinary perhaps, but what you ask is a responsibility I can't take on. Extrapolation is one thing, that's my field. But saying what mortals would feel if they were Gods and on such a delicate issue, well, that is beyond me certainly. Why not hear it from your own, then compare the passions of each side. Yes. That would be the way. To listen to me, well, that would not be sane. I always strive for sanity, if you see what I mean. It's not easy to keep your balance in my line of work. No, this is a task I'd rather not take on, if you please. You see what I mean. Yes, I mean no, this cannot be answered by me."

The crowd of them were bearing down on me now with their eyes alone. I could almost see myself through their eyes, quivering like a blade of grass, knees knocking together under my earthly robes.

"You like sex?" Zeus asked.

"Oh yes," I said too quickly. "I've always liked it."

"See," Zeus said. "The lad is reliable. Well, we can't say he's actually young, not a lad as human beings go. He understands the importance of passion in a life—no matter how long the life goes on. Some men never flag. I'd wager our Teiresias is in the stronghold of this realm. You've still got sex in your life? You make it a point to partake of it?"

"Well, yes," I, a mere seer and mortal man, said hesitantly out loud. "I wouldn't feel whole if I didn't."

"Ha," Zeus said. "You might have been one of my own sons with an attitude like that."

"Yes," I said. But Hera was scowling at me. "Or no. I guess I'm not though. I guess we all know my origins, you fathered my own father's line." I was not about to mention my other connections with Zeus. Even my own mother had known none of it.

"Yes, indeed," Athena said, staring at me to see would I or would I not make an embarrassment of my long-deceased mother and, by extension, of her as well. Her eyebrow cocked over one terrifying eye. My father had already met up with her and found himself skewered to the ground.

"And," Hera said too quietly, "you remember, don't you, Teiresias, when you saw the snakes coupling in the grass and drove them apart? You remember what happened then? You remember how I turned you into a woman for interfering with nature like that?"

"Yes," I said, "I remember it."

"And you remember what it was to have sex and Emporous's children after that. You haven't forgotten, have you?"

"Oh no," I said. "I haven't forgotten it." I could have kicked myself for how timid and childlike I had become in the face of their pointed questioning. But my quiverings were not only from fear, I had to admit, in fairness to myself. It was very cold where I stood at the crest of Mount Olympos. I was shaking in my boots.

"Tell us now, what was it like being a woman suddenly? Being on the receiving end of everything? Tell us exactly what it felt like making the switch."

"Oh no," I said. "I'd rather not. I'd rather not talk about personal, intimate things—in such an important forum, I mean. I've always kept these things to myself. It has been an essential part of my integrity, of my bearing, if you see what I mean, as a man not to talk about my so-called experiences. I—"

"Halt!" Zeus bellowed at me. I turned to see the God of thunder and lightning, of all the heavens and of the world as well, God of home, hearth, hospitality, of liberty, law and order, of property, and of course fertility, blazing with fury about the eyes and mouth. It was not surprising the Gods felt the need to gather in groups against him rather than approach him alone. Each word shook the stones upon which I stood. "This is not a human court!" his voice rang out.

"No," I whispered. "It is certainly not a human court."

"Give us your story. With detail. And make it quick."

"With detail?" I squeaked. I had taken to twisting the hem of my robe in my hand against my leg. "With detail?" I asked again.

"Yes," he said. "We are not children here. A little adult entertainment would do us good. We are very bored these days."

"Yes, indeed," the Gods were saying. "Yes, indeed." Athena was scowling pointedly at me as if to say, "Blow this and your mother will strike you dead if I do not do so myself."

"Excuse me?" Zeus said. "What are you muttering about, boy? Stop muttering and get down to it."

"Nothing, oh nothing," I said. "It was just a phrase, two really, that popped into my mind, a couple of phrases. I've no idea what they're all about. I have some idea, but it wouldn't be appropriate. No, it wouldn't interest you at all. No, I'll just pass that one by."

"What is this 'sweetjesus and buddha'?" Zeus asked, interested now.

"Oh no, it's just a phrase, something silly from the future no

31

doubt," I said hurriedly. "I'll tell you what it's like to be a seer, if you're interested, that is. One of the occupational hazards of being a seer is that you are absolutely flooded with phrases and images that have no connection in the current world. They make no sense at all to anyone except yourself. In fact, they do not make sense, without all the trappings of a real world, without a context, to me either. If you see what I mean." I stalled for time.

Zeus was silent then, and all the rest of them. His gold eyes could show such compassion and deadly power at the same time. The tension was electrifying. With his fingernails Zeus was drumming rolls of thunder in horrifying crashes out across the southern plains. Beside him Hera was smiling quietly. The rest of them were looking on, now keenly interested in what I might say further.

"Go on, 'sweetjesus and buddha' . . . ," Zeus prompted me.

"Well," I said. "All right. I'll stop stalling. I can see it's detail you want. You want to talk about sex. Let's see—"

"Yes," said Hera. "Now that is what we brought you up here for. Tell us what it was like when you changed. That is the part that interests me."

"Yes," I said, now relieved. Surely it was better to talk about sex than to talk about the complete displacement of the world as they knew it and themselves. Certainly. "*Well,*" I said again, jumping in. "When I made the change, at first there was a peculiar feeling throughout my body as if all my cells had been turned inside out."

"Cells!" Zeus bawled. "What are cells? Is this another of your verbal tricks? Use common terminology. How are we to understand what it's all about?"

"He means all the minuscule parts of the body," Hera said. "Don't get so infernally upset. Go on now, Teiresias, tell us everything."

"Ah—well," I said again. Zeus gave me a very cold stare out the tops of his eyes. I had encountered those eyes before, in an entirely different context. "When it happened, all the minuscule parts of the body, even smaller than the fingernails and parts of parts of parts of everything, had the feeling they were being turned inside out. Do you know what it feels like to turn suddenly upside down and then right side up again in the water, whirling around, like a fish?"

"No," Hera said frostily. "I have never felt anything like that feeling."

"I have," Poseidon said. As always, he wore a wreath of moisture in his hair.

"And I," said Athena, carefully watching me, and not protectively either. No, there was malice there. I was certain of that.

"And I," Zeus said. "I have felt the whirling feeling."

"Well, of course you have, Zeus," Hera complained. "You've been a fish any number of ridiculous times."

"Well, have you ever played ringstick, or tumbled in the road? No, I guess not. Well, it was like that," I said hurriedly, trying to finish the conversation before it had begun, "down to the smallest part of me, whirling yet in place, and then that which was outside popped in—and that which was flat, well, it popped out. It was as simple as that."

"What did it feel like when it popped in?" Mnemosyne, the Goddess of memory, asked.

"There was a certain heat, not unlike in ordinary passion, or in nursing a child—" Now Hera was smiling. "It was like that. A certain feeling of well-being and a terror of a force—with heat. Yes, it was extraordinary. Everything was pulsating. I am thankful to have had it go both ways. Turning into a woman and turning back. I will always be thankful to Hera for that. I was going inside someone and being entered all at once. In the same part. It was incredible," I said, carried away now by Mnemosyne's smile.

"Aha!" Hera said. "So you do remember it. Tell us now which way was best."

"Well, yes," I said, gathering momentum against my better judgment, as I have always been wont to do. "Well," I said, slowing down and trying to gauge my accuracy—as if, in the situation, accuracy could really count. "If—" the foolishness of my truthfulness rose up, "if all the pleasure of sex could be divided into ten parts—"

"Yes," Hera said quietly.

"Well, you yourself know, as the Goddess of marriage, how extraordinarily good it is. I don't have to explain it to you."

"Yes, go on," Hera said noncommitally. Later on I would remember how her eyebrow had actually cocked at me.

"Well, if the pleasure in sex is divided into ten parts," I said, thinking—well, at least we are not talking religion here, not with the likes of them. "Well," I said, "then I would have to say that nine parts of the pleasure belong to—"

The silence of the moment was terrifying, I had never heard such a void. "Well," I gulped. "The nine parts belong to the woman, of course. The difference is incredible. I could never have believed it myself, until I experienced it. Perhaps it accounts for how many times a man goes looking for sex. In one session, a woman receives nine times as much."

"In one *session*!?" Hera yowled. "How can you talk like that, when you have been a woman? In one *session*? How can you be so cold? How could you say women have nine parts?" She rose up like a gigantic white-robed ox in front of me. Her skirts went on and on, up and up, towering over me. "You've borne two children and you say women have the better of it—even to nine parts!?"

"But I wasn't looking at childbirth as part of the act," I exclaimed. "That would put an entirely different tone on it. That would make the sexual act nine months in itself. No one has sustained a sexual act for nine months. That is something I venture to say not even a God has done." I looked at Hera's rage and then I corrected myself. "With a mortal, I mean. Of course, Gods have done it for three hundred years or so. Like you," I stumbled. "With Zeus. Everybody knows that. I told you I couldn't speak for Gods in this."

"Childbirth *is* part of the sexual act," Hera, Goddess of child-birth, decreed. "And it is not something that makes for pleas-antries, I'll remind you of that one. It is not nine parts pleasure!

Or even one! Only the end of childbirth, the absence of the act, can give any woman pleasure, and that is because of the pain—the release from it, not the experience, you lout. How can you, supposedly a wise man, divorce the plant from the seed?"

Athena looked thoroughly satisfied for some reason, as if all her suspicions about my male ancestors and my subsequent ability to reason had been borne out. I, Teiresias, looked around myself. It was a moment for which I would have given anything later on to remember clearly—for all the things seeing and unseen, for all the brilliant light and the way it played about the features of Gods and world alike. "It never occurred to me," I said, "that there might be a connection between plant and seed, between the sexual act and the little child. It's something I myself have never heard discussed, much less mentioned even as an hypothesis."

"Good grief," Hera, Goddess of marriage and childbirth, said. "Intelligence among human beings is certainly relative. You are a complete disgrace to the company of Gods." And in one fell swoop she held both my eyes in her hand. I myself, I believe—for a second I could see them sitting there, staring back at me. For one instantaneous horrific moment I saw myself without my own eyes. The rest of it took place as if in slow motion, though it must have happened very rapidly in actuality. First there seemed to be a strip missing from left to right across everything I saw, followed by its return, and then the fragmenting of everything I saw, as if all the world I could see was perched behind an oval glass that had been knocked into pieces and many of the pieces were falling out. One by one they fell until there was no more vision for me. Hera the Goddess had blinded me. And the world of Gods and men and women was completely gone. I stood momentarily struck dumb by the lack of anything at all around me as she set instead two round stones, cold as marbles, inside my head.

I peered out from inside myself without result. There seemed to be a residual flashing of background lights for a few moments as my eyes began to adjust to the distinct void. I could hear them bickering somewhere out there, perhaps very near to me, but I cared even less than I had cared before. I had turned inward now. Now I lived in a nightmare world. "Where have I gone?" I wailed. "Where is everything? Where are all you quarreling ridiculous powerful things?!"

I might as well have been calling into a giant shell by the sea. For no one answered me. And when I held the thought of it to my ear, all I heard was the roar of eternity. There might as well have been only one God now, I thought. For all I knew, or cared. Well, at least it might be a compassionate God, I thought in a morose attitude, for all the good its going to do me now—in this very dark world.

"Well, well," I said to myself, already jabbering and swinging from mood to mood in the abyss, almost giddily, as if I were a child again, swinging at the top of a poplar tree. "It could have been worse," I said, perhaps out loud.

"Oh shut up," Hera hooted somewhere above.

"I only have one request," I said as if shouting from the bottom of a pail.

"Oh, give him his one request," Zeus thundered above. "After all, you've blinded him."

"Please, if you please—send my eyes on to someone else. I can think of a few people who will be needing my eyes before I have a chance to join up with them in the Underworld."

"Why, who is that?" Hera cried. "Who will be needing your eyes?"

"Oh stop," Zeus said. "Leave well enough alone. Let the poor man go home. Haven't you done enough in one day?"

And then there was the sound of gigantic shuffling as the Gods moved back their chairs and slipped away. Oedipos tells me he used the eyes for a time, but was somewhat disappointed to find that in the Underworld there wasn't much to see. "Who's Oedipos?" Hera said at the time. "There's no one on earth yet born who goes by such a preposterous name. What does it mean?" she said. "Who would call their child Engorged Foot? What kind of parental attitude can that be?"

And I, in that moment so very long ago, felt, along with my stunned terror, a sort of relief. Although I could no longer see anyone or anything, I knew that if they had asked me again the more delicate questions, the questions referring to the worship of Gods by human beings, or even about my own relationship to Zeus, which had inadvertently been raised, then surely I would have been killed or tortured. Silently I thanked Zeus for holding his tongue and thought upon the fates of many Gods and mortals alike. But for a momentary absentmindedness of Gods on this day, I might have turned out like poor Prometheus, who had only tried to help man progress a bit by giving him fire for his food and work. Where was Prometheus now? Because of Zeus, poor Prometheus in all his waking hours was having his liver eaten out by birds while chained to a rock, arms and legs stretched backward painfully, belly exposed. During the night he was subject to his body's own painful healings, which could afford him no sleep, before the birds started in on him again. Yes, I was lucky to have fallen to the anger of Hera rather than Zeus, I thought. There were so many others this God Zeus had put to his penalties, although his wife, too, had been relentless in her cruelties when the fidelity of Zeus was in question or at stake. Yes, I thought, I am lucky to have merely been blinded when I think of the last time I encountered Zeus. Yes, what would Hera have thought of that intimate act? I would have been lucky to get to the Underworld at all.

"Yes, yes," I said aloud. "I'll just be tottering home. If only someone out there will give me a hand."

My mother's house was set at the edge of town near a stand of trees. We who saw the mountains all around us but only from a distance looked upon this thicket in the flatlands as a forest. Forest, we said, when directing others to our house. It was only natural that we should live here. My mother was Athena's nymph, and it was said that the Goddess frequented that spring which rose up in our woods like encouragement and swelled into a flowered pond. Each morning our maids would receive from the men and women of Thebes the sacrifices to Athena at our front door, and the gifts that supported us. And it was out the back door that I went when I first awaked.

I did not know whether it was the overwhelming smell of humus emanating from our backyard that led me out, the embarrassment of being so admired by the celebrants if I should go out the other door, or my growing affection for the dark-haired servant girl who made my bed each morning and who, if asked, would bathe me each and every day long into my old age. There was nothing better in the world, I thought, than to root among the tender undergrowth in search of sticks and brush for the morning baking, and to hear in the distance the sound of birds and my mother's gentle humming as mortal and God lay together entangled in the far reaches of our backyard. I knew Leiriope, our neighbor to the west, would be looking out from her window, her delicate skin as blue as that pond beside which my mother lay in rapture.

It was said that the River Kephissos had embraced this neighbor on its way to Lake Kopais, that it had taken her under its tumultuous surface and made love to her until her flesh turned as blue as the iris of one radiant, staring eye. This humiliation had taken place in Phokis, from which Leiriope then fled, or so people said. Here in Thebes she dwelled on that memory, far away from the place of its occasion, here where people did not falsify the facts in the marketplace and make remarks about love's tumultuous waters practically at the lobe of her tender ear. Often I would see her blue hand rise up in that window overlooking our woods. Each morning her blue hand would wave, and then her blue voice would fall gently down upon me in greeting, not unlike my own mother's call. Something melancholy would rise up in me then, even as a child, and I could not help the blue tear that sprang each morning out of my eye when Leiriope called my name.

I did not know for some time that Leiriope had a son, for he did not often go out of the house. It was said that the river had fathered him, and his olive skin was smooth as a pebble at the bottom of a stream. His eyes were not blue; they were black as Leiriope's, and were said to start the hearts of children and adults (men and women alike) aflame as if they had been pieces of flint for people to strike their bodies against.

It was a custom that no man should take a boy to be his pupil before that boy had sprung his first down from his chin; and yet all the elders and the king, too, it was rumored, had courted him. They brought him little presents, setting him on their knees and stroking his sleek hair, letting their fingers wander into the hollows of his cheeks, along his child lips. But he would not respond. He sat—not angry, not the slightest bit irritated, and certainly not in love with them. He was the pebble itself before the persons sitting there. He did not cry out, or murmur; he sat silent as a chair while his gifts piled up. Often the women would fondle him, too, crying out: Tiny Beauty, Perfect Skin. He was nine and I seven when I, too, fell in love with him.

It is true that children in their own ways often fall in love with one another, but my feeling for Narcissus was not the same as that. How does one love another who gives no response? Passionately, I say. More and more—projecting one's own feeling as the sentiments of the other, saying that that person must feel as I feel for he will not deny it. It is nothing more than self-love in the end; and what can be more enticing, more destructive than that? There are situations, but they are few and terrifying to think about.

One day, inexplicably, Narcissus started coming from his house each day to sit in the woods, near where Helen, our maid, and I went to gather kindling. He had, I think, been driven from his own house (even the kitchen, the courtyard, his own room) by the persistence of his suitors. A little arbor had grown up in the woods like a cave, and that was how I first saw him—crouched in view of our back door, casting pebbles against a fallen nut-tree. My arms were already full up to my chin with branches, which I intended to break down behind our house into more manageable pieces for the hearth, and Helen had gone back to prepare my mother's morning cakes while I searched for the continual one more twig to add to the fire.

I stopped suddenly before him, staring unkindly. "Whatever has made your hair so silver?" I blurted out. His hair shone out the color of an aging man's, but with luster. His one eye was set in his head just slightly higher than the other. I knew immediately who he was, though later out of politeness I would ask him. No, he was not beautiful as they had said, I thought then. Certainly I was as compelling. I had the same black hair —though mine was not streaked as his was. My skin was soft, too, like a fawn's ears, but my eyes, I knew, did not seem to drift ever so slightly one from the other.

"Well then," I said, watching him looking at me—not with suspicion. No, he was not suspicious. It was as if he did not care what it was that I would say. "If you won't answer my question, will you tell me your name?" I could have said anything and his eyes would have been just as disengaged.

His voice was not unusual; it was neither high nor low; it did not break yet between childhood and manliness. He said his name when he said Narcissus. Shyly he said it. Or perhaps I only thought it shyness, for I felt it myself as I watched him pitching stones halfheartedly at the nut-tree. Although he did not invite me to sit down with him, I let my bundle of sticks fall with a crash to one side of us. "I live over there," I said, squatting down beside him under the tangled branches. I, too, pitched a stone toward the nut-tree as he looked toward our house and nodded.

"I have silver hair because my father took my mother on a gray day; the sun had just come out from behind a cloud," he murmured, digging in the dirt for a particular stone. The choice of stones was all important in pitching. We both knew that; that was unspoken.

"My father is a shade," I said matter-of-factly, for he had

been so for as long as I could remember—at least when I was awake.

"My father is a river," he said. "A God," he said proudly. "Whenever I want I can see my father, whenever someone will take me there. I remember when I was born, too."

"You do?" I said, looking askance at him.

"I do," he said. "I floated up from the river into a hollow cave where I got my silver hair, and then I fell into the world smiling. I was smiling when I was born."

"How do you know you were smiling?" I asked him. We were pitching another round of stones. "Only someone else could have seen that. Maybe you heard someone tell about your smile. Maybe you only thought you remembered it yourself."

"I felt it," he said. "I felt myself smile."

I smiled off into the open space beyond the thicket where we crouched. I tried to feel it. "Yes," I said, "I see what you mean."

"I haven't smiled since," he said.

"Maybe you should gather wood with Helen and me," I said. "That always makes me smile. I smile, too, when I see your mother in the window. Then I cry."

"I haven't any reason to smile," he said.

"I could make you smile. I make Helen smile when we gather wood, and my mother, too, when I holler in my bath. I could holler. Would that make you smile?"

"No," he said. "Did you know King Kadmos comes to see me?"

"Does he try to make you smile?"

"No. He tries to make himself smile. Everyone wants me for his pupil. Everyone thinks I'm beautiful. My father is a God."

"Lots of people's fathers are Gods," I said. "That doesn't make anyone think you're beautiful. Why, lots of people have Gods for fathers. There are bunches of them right on our street. Besides," I said, looking at him, "I think you're kind of plain. Your right eye looks like it might drift right out of your face."

"It does?" he asked, looking at me for the first time. He closed his right eye. "Does that help? Maybe I have my one eye closed when they look at me and call me beautiful. Does it help?"

"No," I said. "Try the other one."

He closed his left eye.

"Now open them both," I said. "I think you're better with your eyes open—even if one does look like it might drift right out of your face."

There was a little twig in his hair and I went to brush it out, but he raised his hand to block my arm. "Nobody touches me," he said.

"Nobody?" I asked.

"Nobody."

"Not your mother?"

"No."

"Not your maid?"

"Nobody."

"What about King Kadmos then? He must at least put his hand in your hair. You couldn't refuse to be touched by the king."

"I don't feel it. I was born in Phokis," he said. "I fell into Phokis smiling. My eyes aren't crooked."

"They are. Your right eye is higher than the other. But, you know, it really isn't plain. A minute ago I thought that, but now I think it isn't plain. It isn't beautiful, but it isn't plain. Plain would be if they were straight like anybody else's. Are you bored?"

"What?"

"Are you bored? Your eyes don't look bored; it's the rest of your face."

"I have a cat," he said. "Do you want to see my cat?"

"What kind of cat is it?" I asked.

"A boring cat, but I can show it to you. Its name is River Willow."

"I have to take the kindling in now," I said. "But I can see your cat after that." I stood up and began to reassemble my stack of sticks. "Do you want to come along? Then we could see your cat."

"No." He chucked another stone.

"All right," I said. "I'll come back. Will you still be here?"

"Most likely," he said. "Most probably I will."

Finally my mother had convinced the blue Leiriope to make the journey with us. We would travel—my mother and I, Narcissus, Leiriope, and several of our maids—to Delphi. We would go slightly out of our way so that Leiriope could visit the banks of Kephissos, which she had not seen since she had given birth to Narcissus. Here, too, Narcissus might know heritage. At Delphi each of us would, that next day, ask the pythia one question. I had had considerable trouble selecting only one, but I would turn eight soon and I was certain that, with my new age, I would be better able to think about whatever it was I wanted to know. Narcissus would not say what his question was, and I had no opportunity to ask Leiriope for hers. Helen, when asked, merely threw the cooking towel she wore around her waist up over her head.

My mother alone would confide in me. She would ask the pythia, she said, what her future would be. When I asked her why she did not ask the oracle what the Gods planned for me instead, as the other mothers did for their sons, she stared at me as if I had just become a stone. "Would you crawl back into my womb, Teiresias?" she asked quite harshly. When I said that I would not, she replied, "Well, then." This perplexed me for some time. (It was not until I myself had become a woman and a mother that I understood, and then I understood it only by degrees until I heard myself actually saying it.)

Each morning I found Narcissus in his cave. All I could speak of was the approaching journey to the great crevice where the future was said to speak, where all of the world had begun to turn for counsel. As for Narcissus, he seemed to have no interest in that part of our excursion.

There had been some conversation between Leiriope and my

mother about the need for protection. We had not ascended into the wealthy ranks of the chariot-owners, and so we would be walking for twelve days altogether. There was said to be some danger of marauders, though they did not frequently venture inland, and the thought of this quite terrified Leiriope. If we should meet up with any sort of adversity, my mother told her, we would call upon Athena. At this remark, Leiriope was instantly reassured. What better protection could she have had than that of the Goddess of wisdom and peace. My mother's relationship with that Goddess was not unknown in any part of the world as far as anyone we knew could determine.

On the night before our departure, my mother took great pains to alleviate Leiriope's self-consciousness about wandering into Phokis, where her blue skin had become legendary. The people in her homeland could not restrain themselves from looking at the way her sullen eyelids came down over the white of her eyes, the way her beautiful blue lips were set off by her teeth. They could not keep themselves from looking; they could not keep from looking away. And so, on this final evening, the lamps were lighted. The maids from our house and Leiriope's had been called into my mother's sitting room. Paints of every color, of the least and greatest expense, had been accumulated; all around the room palettes and pots and brushes were strung like beads in orderly rows, and at the center stood Leiriope stripped bare of all her clothes. Narcissus and I sat quietly together in one large chair—for how could we be anything but quiet with one another? Narcissus would not say a word. The maids were chatting wildly about what should be done, while upstairs my mother rushed about dragging chests and boxes across the floor. When she came into the room, her softest paintbrush in her hand, a silence fell. Leiriope crossed her arms over her breasts, turned toward the window, toward the door.

"Ah," sighed my mother, seeing her friend. Leiriope's back swept down in a luminous curve, her spine a thread of cobalt pearls. Her buttocks were smooth, slightly hollowed from her loss of weight, like delicate shells. Out from under her narrow collarbone, under the thin crossed arms, a crescent of breast appeared and under that the cascade of little ribs, her sloping belly and thin hipbones like wings above the blue-black tuft of hair. "So," my mother said, admiring her, perhaps even more than the rest of us were doing now. "So the new hairless cult has not taken you in," she said.

Leiriope hid her slight smile with her hand. It was rumored around that the women in the palace had started removing all their body hair. They had begun, it was said, with the plucking of the soft hairs on their hands and toes. Next had come the thighs and shins, until finally the people said there was not a hair left on the women at the palace save on their heads—not on their knees, beneath their arms, or between their legs. The queen, her daughters, and all the women of the court had plucked themselves bald in a self-destructive rage. Soon, the common people said, there would be a profession made of it. Slaves would be trained to tweeze the little hairs one by one from each female torso and limb. Even now it was reported that the women surrounding the king were pouring hot wax on one another in order to more easily "rip the devoted moss from the stone which would be freed." Narcissus and I could see that our mothers thought it a great joke. Half the maids were burrowing under one of the curtains as if it were a skirt, mock tweezers in hand. "No! Whee!" the others squealed, tossing the draperies up and down.

What were the colors they placed on the body of the meek Leiriope? The deep green of the turtle, the turquoise of the peacock's feathered eye, the soft gray of the swallow's down. Vermilion, amethyst, the royal cadmium. And under all of it, under the circles, squares, and swirls, lay a coat of the finest gilt. From head to toe she wore a golden crown. Even her blue hairs were coated with Egyptian reds and greens. We watched her strutting boldly back and forth as if she were none other than herself reborn to an even more exaggerated skin. The maids stared on to see her there—the sad and small Leiriope had thrown her shoulders back. Her small breasts bobbed like two jeweled purses on her chest as she strode from windowpane to windowpane looking into the wild reflection of herself. Only when she opened her eyes up wide could we see that slightest blue at the insides of her eyelids. From window to window she spun, flinging out her arms in gestures we had never seen, laughing wildly to herself.

"Funereal seal!" my mother cried.

The gold face turned and fell. "What is it?" Leiriope's hands fluttered up to her spectacular, beaded cheeks.

"It's all wrong! Every bit of it!"

Leiriope drew her glided fingers up toward her wrists as if to hide them in her nonexistent sleeves. "Remove all this!" my mother commanded. I felt Narcissus grip my arm. I do not know even now whether he was touched by his mother's flight into ecstasy and tormented by her fall, or whether he had found in his mother some beauty or release from shame that he had never experienced before. He sat staring on, saying nothing as we watched the blue tear drop from her eye and nestle briefly on her golden collarbone. Down it ran, tingeing the path to the ebony-tipped breast, resting there and dropping onto her belly. My mother walked quietly over to her friend; she put one finger under the golden chin and turned the painted face toward hers. "Little Lily," she said, looking into the dark and overflowing eyes. I saw my mother's other hand then cup itself around the brittle painted hairs between Leiriope's golden thighs as if to cradle Leiriope where the God had wounded her. My mother's eyes did not leave Leiriope's and Leiriope did not look away.

In that instant Leiriope's shoulders ceased their heaving, her eyes cleared, and she flung her arms around my mother as a child might have done, as I myself wanted to do. In a single breath, the maids sighed.

"We will start over," my mother said, "if that's all right with you, Lily." Leiriope once again turned her eyes up toward my mother and nodded. I heard her say, "Thank you, Chariklo." It seemed odd to me to hear my mother's given name spoken, as it always did when I was a child.

The following morning we started out. On Leiriope there was no paint anywhere save on her chest, where she wore like a pendant above her breasts the symbol ΣiMí painted delicately in the gold that had overpowered her so. It was a word I would not understand until one night many years later when Emporous and his reluctant scribe sat scratching it in stone.

As we went along, the maids divided into two groups. Helen and two of Leiriope's attendants walked on ahead of us, while three of our maids followed in our wake. I always liked to hear them discussing the kitchen and bedroom, worlds that then seemed large to me. At the center of our procession walked my mother and Leiriope. Leiriope carried a bundle of dried water flowers she had kept beside her bed for years, or so Narcissus said when I prodded him. It was Leiriope's intention, Narcissus said, to toss these flowers into the river God's hair.

Narcissus and I stepped along directly behind our mothers, our sandals swinging over our shoulders, accompanied by the huge cat that Narcissus had said was boring. Its head was larger than the shoulders it sat upon, and out of its striped face stared two immense green eyes. It had a short yellow tail, no longer than my own hand, that stuck straight up above its white rear. It marched directly at Narcissus's side as though it had been born a puppy. Every once in a while we would hear it speak in the same small aspiring voice that the town rooster had. I had never owned a puppy or the white-breasted weasels people kept to hold on their laps and stroke. As it padded along beside us, I grew exultant that this one cat, River Willow, had escaped the furriers, that it had not gone the way of other cats. But I grew irritated, too, that this stocky animal should give so much obeisance to Narcissus, who attended to no one at all.

During the second day, I had heard my mother saying to Leiriope that she thought Leiriope should turn of her own accord from her thoughts of Kephissos, that she should not carry these devotions further once she had been at the river again. Leiriope had cried at that as she walked slowly along, weighted down by the thought of it, at the borders of the lake. In a few months the lake would be nearly dry again, returned to marshland as it did each year in the latter part of spring. That small island toward which Leiriope now turned her eyes would no longer be a spot of green in that sweep of blue; it would be, until winter came again, merely a part of the vast morass. As she turned it was almost as if she had been swallowed up by that lake and its source, so similar was the color of the water and her flesh. I could see only the light dress she wore, her sandals, and the inscription on her chest. My mother took her hand and they went on ahead of us up the beach. I could see her shoulders shaking in front of me, and I stepped up and took hold of her skirt, following along that way for some time, her other hand lying over the top of my head and forehead like a cap of sky.

That night we put down our bedding at the edge of the lake, just as we had on the first night. We prayed that Athena would keep an eye on our procession and tried to fall directly to sleep. I lay cuddled up with River Willow on my belly until Narcissus called to it and it shot to his side on the other side of the fire. Leiriope lay some distance from me, but still I could see her tossing and turning there on the night before we would reach the Kephissos. On the other side of me rested my mother, and all around us lay the maids, chatting quietly until they, too, nodded off. By night and by day we made a long journey, each in our separate ways.

Leiriope stands on the cliff above the Kephissos. My mother holds us back. Narcissus is crying: he wants to see his father, he wails. He is biting and kicking the maids. Over the edge Leiriope is throwing the deadened branches she has carried with her since the day when she opened her eyes under these waters and knew pain. We are below her, below the cliff, downstream. That *is* your father, Helen says. Hush up. The branches float, whirl in an eddy, are sucked under. Leiriope throws her veils, her scarves. We see the yellow scarves float down, catch at a willow, smother the stream briefly. The rings make, for a moment, two small holes in our grief as we hear her above. No one understands her words. She has taken the ivory-handled knife from her basket. We see it white as teeth in her hand. She is cutting her hair. *I want to see my father.* Helen slaps his wailing face. *My father will kill you,* he screams. *My father will rape you and turn you blue like mold.* Leiriope leans precariously over the edge. She is shouting, she is wailing. No one knows what she has said. My mother holds me back. My mother calls the name she has given her. *Lily.* Hair floats down like petals onto the rapidly flowing stream. Leiriope is tugging at her hand. Her back turns toward us. We hear her yelling now. It is a cry of relief. We all look up. Something sparkles in the sunlight and falls. We see it plummet. The maids turn their heads away. They cover their faces with their hands. There—in a shallow between two rocks—is Leiriope's blue finger caught in the osculating mouth of an eel's thin, slippery skin.

Up and up we went along the path where the mountain ruptured itself into that place they called Delphi. Leiriope walked on ahead of us, humming without variation, her bandaged hand held out in front of her as if it were her own pale shadow. Narcissus had had to be dragged away from the banks of the Kephissos. Now he languished on the litter the maids had been forced to draw behind them. One arm he had thrown up over his head in sulky consternation, the other he wrapped around the absurdly loyal River Willow. I looked at them there—clamped tightly together. I would gladly have taken either's place to have been part of such a union. The great furry mass was stretched out on its back, its striped tail between its hefty thighs, the immense head secured like a turnip on Narcissus's shoulder. Narcissus's eyes had shut me out, as had River Willow, content in its violent purring. I hated them both.

I had been trying not to think about that question which I had not yet formulated for the oracle. My own indecisiveness now hounded me. Should I not, at my advanced age—I was eight now, was I not?—should I not be able to think of one question? Infants had been to the oracle, stammered the right syllables and rhythms, and gone home with their entire lives charted before them. The problem lay in the restriction. Two questions would have been far more reasonable than one, three than two, I thought, counting out each of my ridiculous ideas on my fingers. My pointer finger with the little nick on it where once I cut myself, where I had first discovered blood, would be the first. Would I have, like the charioteers, a tunic spun all in silver threads, gold armbands up and down both tremendous arms, a bronze dagger inlaid with a muscled lion? I followed the finger up my arm to my own sallow, skinny bicep. The second question would come from the middle finger, which I often raised in salute as the other boys did. Would I have a cat—no! not a dog! But a cat which I myself would save from its usual fate: the imperiled existence of a scavenger until inevitably it was caught and skinned by peddlers in the market-place before the cheering crowds. At this thought, my head refused to turn toward them, toward Narcissus, who had already accomplished this, and the cat who had superseded the destiny of its kind. Against my will, my eyes sneaked in their direction. There they lay, together, content. I held up the finger. It was a noble request to present to the pythia, but it was not enough. Three. This was the finger, they said, that had roots which grew up a person's arm and through the shoulder, down and around into the pounding of the emotions. Walking far ahead of us all, now in her purple gown, was the beautiful Helen; and there on the litter lay the slender body of Narcissus. When I was old enough, would they love me as much as I now loved them? Or would I be chosen as the favorite of the king?

I had what I considered to be three questions now. But I could not think of a fourth any more than I could single out one good one to present. My fingers wagged before me. I didn't need to voice these three possibilities. I could imagine how my mother and Leiriope would smile at one another, and at me, raising their eyebrows momentarily. Their long dresses swayed before me, lifting slightly to show their tightening ankles. Beneath the one skirt the white heels glittered from out of my mother's sandals; beneath the other the blue slivers startled me. I looked at my hands. Perhaps it was just as well that only one question could be asked, for at what number would the limit be set if not at that one? I would have been taken with a serious sadness (perhaps I, too, would have been incapacitated and carried on the litter—to lie with them both; I thought about that possibility for some time) if I had had to see Leiriope hold up what was left of her blue hands in confusion before the pythia and say: "Ten? Ten? But I have only nine questions for you."

It was said all over the world that the oracle could predict the future of anything: the number of grapes that would cling in one summer to a vine as it trembled upward, the exact revolution at which a particular pink moth would soar too near a flame, the day and hour when one stone on the road from Thebes to Athens would be crushed by a passing chariot. My hands trembled and my ankles and knees revolted at the thought of my impending moment before her. I would stand before the greatest of them all, inhaling the scent of sweet myrtle as it emanated from just one of her awesome nostrils, overcome by the unquestionable authority of rotten garlic as she jettisoned that from the other. I would stand there stricken by my own incompetence and say, as I had heard my nighttime father say, the one word: *Well*. But there would be no question to it. I had no questions.

A shaft of light preceded us now, cutting straight up to where the Kastalian Spring circled transparently beside the cave of the pythia. I do not know what happened between the time when I still looked forward to days of traveling and the moment when we stood in front of her, marveling at the oiled surface of her head, the two strands of black hair that ran down her crown and were tucked definitively behind an ear. I watched her flesh rolling as if in waves as she crouched there at the mouth of the cave, sighing repeatedly, eyes closed, apparently waiting for one of us to speak.

One by one the others went ahead of me. The watery eyes opened. Yes, little Helen would marry—a man of her own age—and cast forth seven children—the first two, stones. Leiriope's red-haired maid would die in the flames of passion, the old woman said, but not before she had enjoyed the warmth. I could see the maid tossing her bright hair out of its stays, thinking not of the end but of the pleasure, as the other servants went forward. All but one would have children and bake the finest cakes on the plains, the one with bright hair would lie like a rug before kings. I saw them looking at one another, obviously pleased; even the one who was to be childless before the throne. It was just as my mother had said: the pythia did look like a yellow onion with only the two hairs to interrupt her wisdom. She was truly a great one. And I? I was the smallest of fleas.

It was now my mother's turn. I stood kicking at a stone in anxiety. My mother would speak and listen. Then Leiriope, Narcissus, and I— I would have to say something. The cat was stretched out on the litter in the sun. That would not be a suitable question, I knew as much as that. It had to be something important, but how was I to know importance in my life? I kicked again, and then I heard my mother hiss. I heard my name. She was staring at me, as were Leiriope and every one of the maids. Narcissus had turned in disgust. What makes a cat, too, look at one with all the rest? I drew myself in like a branchless stick. The old woman was staring straight ahead.

"I have this to ask—" my mother said now, clearing her throat as if to rid them all of the thought of my impropriety. I could see her hands clenched tightly behind her back, one finger pointing at me in admonition. "I have borne a son; I am mistress to Athena—"

"Sssisss—" the pythia adjudicated. "I know all that."

"I would like to have a daughter, though I will not couple again with a man."

The pythia's face grew rounder, though she did not actually smile at that moment. Her eyes opened wide. "Ha!" she laughed then. "An entire questionnaire! Who would have expected it?" The corners of my mother's lips went up and then they fell as she glanced around at us.

"You will have a daughter, though you will not bear a daughter. You will not see her face."

"But what does that mean?" my mother stammered looking again at the rest of us.

"Enough," the old woman said. "It pleases me to give an answer to your question equal to the question itself. Stand aside. You have heard the truth."

Leiriope fell on her knees before the oracle even before my mother in her daze had moved at all, before my mother had given up the attempt to collect herself and had slumped down in the dirt. The blue hand was out in front of them, cradling the bandaged one.

"You have healed your hand," the woman said to her. "Sometimes to heal ourselves we must cut ourselves off."

Leiriope's face turned up, her eyes gazing into the closed eyes of the pythia. She began to sob. "Will my sadness never leave me? Will I never be free from all this?"

"One question only! Which one?"

Confused, Leiriope looked down at the dirt on which she and the old woman were crouched; her hands shook in front of her.

"Ah," said the old woman, opening her eyes. "Can't make up your mind. Next."

"No, no, I'll make up my mind. I will."

"Shush," said the old woman. "I will answer your question. Life overtakes us like a series of unexpected assaults. Can we be free, as you say, when this is irrevocably the case?"

Helen, watching this, had clasped hold of the red-haired maid's hand, and the red-haired maid had grabbed on to the hand of yet another of them. Here we were in our fear, and yet the trees rustled quietly, pleasantly overhead.

"Blue Bird!" the pythia said. "I have asked you a question.

You must learn to answer back. That is the only freedom that begets freedom. Will you take it or leave it, Blue Bird?" Leiriope cringed quite visibly as the oracle went on. "What is it in the color blue that scarifies you so? Is blue not the color of the unimpeded sky? Is blue not the color of this coveted eye?" The massive woman drew down her own lower lid and laughed as the blue eye stared out at Leiriope. "Ha! Sky. Eye. I have made a sound that very much pleases me. Is blue your ΣίΜί? Is blue your destiny? I have nearly done it again." She laughed quietly to herself. "You! Blue Bird! do not know the difference between derision and a catalyst to gather strength. Be bold, be bold, be bold, be not too bold. How can a human being be in the world when he thinks only of the size of his nose, or of the place where once a splinter pierced his foot? Listen to Chariklo; she knows something of this."

At this mention of her name, my mother looked up, startled. She and Leiriope gathered themselves together and limped to one side. At this, Narcissus leaped, as though he had never once been disheartened enough to ride the litter all this way, to take their place. "Don't ask me about your father," the old woman said. "And don't ask anyone else."

Narcissus looked at her in astonishment, his one eye riding his forehead like a fly. He thought for a moment and then slowly he closed it. "Don't try to be beautiful," she said. "That will get you nowhere with me."

"But what will I do?" Narcissus said suddenly.

"There is nothing for you to do. The jig is up. As for your cat—he will live a long and happy life." Then the pythia laughed.

My mother shoved me forward then as if to fill up the awkward silence as Narcissus sulked to one side. I was in front of her. I was peering into the mound of flesh with the two closed eyes.

"This is my son Teiresias," my mother said, as I had not said a word.

"No questions from him," the old woman said.

"But I have a question!" I cried, misunderstanding her, for just then I had come upon it. "I have a question for you. I thought I wouldn't, but I do."

Her thin lip curled up in the excess of her face, her eyes narrowed in disgust. "I will hear no questions from *you!*" She spat at the side of my foot.

"But why?" my mother, Helen, and Leiriope cried in one voice.

"Is that another question?"

"No," they said, looking in subjugation toward the ground.

"Then I will answer it," the pythia said. "I will answer this nonquestion for you. I will answer it with a question or two, and then I will go in and have a rest. Here is the question: Why should the young Teiresias ask the onion lady what he already knows? Does the eagle ask the bat how he should see? He knows everything; do you not, young Teiresias?" She spat once again near my heel in disdain. With that she raised herself up, and we watched her suntanned haunches moving slowly into the darkness of the cave.

"Whatever does she mean about my daughter, about *me?*" My mother thrust her hands up to her cheeks. "And you! You—lout!" She whirled furiously toward me. "You think you know everything! She means you are insubordinate!" She boxed me on the ears. Helen and the rest of them would not look at me. I had been scorned by the oracle at Delphi! We left our offerings at the entrance to the cave and turned in our own footprints to make the long journey home. I wandered along behind them all, holding my one question close in my heart. Why death? I asked myself again and again. Why death?

III

Hippopotamos

Together we sit along the Lethe, shades one and all as ever anyone came to be. How is it I alone can recall how it was we passed through another world, I who yet have something further to understand. I tell myself, even after the passing of all these people, this time, that in the telling perhaps I may set it straight, if not in time and circumstance then in a kind of morality of man to man, woman to woman, alien country to alien country, and everything that lies in between.

Settle down now, together on the banks. You have missed the story of the beginning of the world, but then I missed it, too. It is the beginning of my own life I have again begun to tell, and the end, wound around peculiarity in a dream that is as fragmentary as life itself, life that is real and memorable, life where we have always found meaning not in events themselves but somewhere in between.

It has been said that my boy cut my birds to study their innards for prophecies. So goes the speculation of the world, extravagant, cruel, and grotesque. The only birds disemboweled on my behalf were common kitchen fare: chickens, pheasants, doves. Long after I had reached middle age and lost my eyesight, even then, I would turn to my sighted aide to describe it to me: that darting second life that traveled, independently of any winged spirit, along the ground, the shadow of the being itself. In that I found the truest state, the future, too.

The actual disemboweling for prophecy was my lifelong dissection of one dream. Need I recount the merest personal life that surrounded it? the rise and fall of kings and queens? Indeed it fades. We sit with wrinkled shaken paws impelling our walking implements to go backward in our wakeful dreams to a time when we dreamed forward, as if eternally.

Odysseus is beckoning. He is the first fully fleshed human sight Teiresias has seen in who knows how long. The Gods plucked Teiresias's sight before he lived even a quarter of his years. It was restored in the Valley of Death. Now what a gentle vision of Thebes's great warrior: this harsh Odysseus, plunderer of Troy, who was led astray by further want of spoils. Half his men are dead, the other half weak and moaning for home. Odysseus, too, is thin. Out from under the black and white mustache, Odysseus's pink lip trembles as he points toward the bowl of sweet black blood he has been told to offer here. "Please, feel free. Could you—drink blood?" the fearless warrior, awestruck and confused, nods his head of hair toward Teiresias, long dead and longer renowned to all the world. Odysseus's beard is striped good and bad as his ventures are. The beard brushes leather breastplate and armbands, is gray at one side, black, then white, then gray again. Odysseus, alone here, lives.

Of all the shades, Teiresias's memory alone is intact; Teiresias has no need of blood. Yet, even after many odd years dead, he knows that a certain courtesy is preferred. He will pretend to sip to hear this living man speak. Teiresias has become most gracious, an intent host to the newly dead, eking conversation from his guests, secretly frantic in this pursuit. It is two or three hours at best before the memory of each will fail, all cultural reference dissolve. These mothlike wraiths, former women and men of the world, what do they now know?

The one called Odysseus brings news: of how he and his own men made it happen, what Teiresias has known would come to be, the fall of Thebes's companion city, a city called Troy, the City of Grace. And Odysseus's subsequent misfortunes, of these Odysseus speaks. "All the senseless wanderings," Odysseus says. From out of the knotted shawl that grows from Odysseus's face, his piercing hawk eyes survey first one way and then the next. His voice is trembling then, as he peers—perhaps toward escape. "Excuse me, I have never seen such sights as these." He waves his heavy, scarred, and deeply weather-tanned hand.

It is for Teiresias as if he is seeing the Underworld for that first time: when the old fanged dog howled and the raft was slippery under his feet. Down the river he'd been propelled, standing thus, his hood pulled tight around his face and the vibration of pounding waves quite wild beneath. "Why this hood, ferrier?" he'd growled. "Don't you know—I cannot see?"

But no answer came. For the first time in he didn't know how long, he felt himself to be newly blinded, ageless, as if it were he himself who could not be seen. Waves came and went, systematically rocked and jarred him, in insubstantial seas.

When the string was let loose at his chin, the hood fell from his face as his foot touched down. In just that same moment, his dead eyes fell wide open as his hood, there to see! A grateful sight. Something stood before his eyes, drawn long with grief. A body of gray water fell over a jagged cliff, tumbled down, went round in a deep pool of haze, and slowed in front of him. Rocks, water, the pebbled bottom without variegation, stones no bigger than his fingertips. Flowers burned in a mass up one hillside, and some growing things, vegetation of some sort, myriad anemone, clear clear water, deep but clear to the path of pebbles underneath, round and flat each tiny stone, worn down. "Yes!" he said, more to himself than to the ferrier, who was already poling the raft away. "I can see!" But it was not long until he realized that the sights he remembered from his childhood and youth were richer than these. There was little light here. Trees were a mass of green, no illumination cut them into the serration of leaves. No individual petals burst the world into a textured place. And what were these wafting shades of former men and women, children, too? How vague this new world. A deadening silence fell over him.

He remembered it well. How the shades had brushed against him then, and he had imagined them, projected it onto them—his gladness at their accompaniment. He cast his thoughts upon them, almost glowing before him, ring of charity and light. "Drink," they'd coolly said.

Together on their knees they'd bent along the riverbank, the great willows bowing down in infinite haze. It was as if someone played one lingering low note on the flute. The asphodel made a yellow halo of the far hill to one side. The see-through persons cupped their pastel hands and drew the river into them by way of their eternal lips. *Drink, so that you might forget. We have forgotten, too.*

He leaned down to take the nurture. But when he sat back on his heels, he was not new like them, not radiant, not vague. The hounds of his past and all the ones he had conjured yet to come, they were just as real. They knew it, too, as they looked at him. For there was no transformation in his voice. He held out his hand for assistance getting up. It was said then that he had lived far too long for the benefit of death now to take effect in him.

But how long ago had that been? Now again someone offered to quench his thirst.

"Yes, drink blood," Odysseus encouraged an ancient Teiresias, holding out his hand. One of Odysseus's knuckles was prematurely swollen, gnarled. "Circe said I should offer this to you." Odysseus's thighs and arms jutted out from beneath tunic and breastplate, sinewy, brown.

Teiresias shifted uncomfortably, afloat forever now in his hooded robe, his voice a wanderer in its own throat: here it weaves crackling upward, suddenly down. The skin on his face and throat, his hands, a similarly undefined thing. He strokes his nearly hairless head under cover of his hood, and stares. "I lose track. How long were you lost, Odysseus?"

"I count it infinitely." Odysseus's eyes fixed upon the ghostly feet of the most famed wise one. "I've made mistakes."

"Ah. Look at me." How bright the eyes of the living man he sees. "I've heard what others think your merits are. How would you cite them?"

"I would not." Around the iron and leather breastplate, the warrior's sunburned chest.

"Don't be coy now."

The lined and haggard face of Odysseus started. His eyes were stern upon the ancient man. His pink lips tightened in the opening of his beard. "Coy? Of course not. What do you wish to know?"

"What were your mistakes, Odysseus?"

"Mistakes!" Odysseus stared at the only one who could show him the way. "All right, call them mistakes. They have made my life, warp and weft, all that has been good."

Again the soft voice. "What are they?"

Odysseus leaned against the granite ledge. "All right—*greed*." Old Teiresias did not say a word. "You want to know what else, I suppose? *Lust*. Insatiable lustiness gnawed my root. I itched with it. It took over my mind. I lost some of my men—but you must know! *Narrow-mindedness*. Why do you make me say it? Others went far further than I. Agamemnon had himself a daughter he killed—"

An eerie reminder from the depths of the hooded robe. For the captain of the ship: "We're talking about you." Teiresias closed his eyes.

"Humbly, I've come to ask the way home."

"I know that, Odysseus."

"Circe said—"

"Your young sailor Elpenor is swift-footed. Before the ladder from which he fell hit the ground, he was weeping information about your escapades. Let's converse."

"I'm not much for talk. Wind and water—"

"Tell me about the birds you've seen then."

"The birds?"

"Yes, along the way."

"For an augury, I see."

"No, I've missed them very much. That and the smell of human sweat. All my life I thrilled at every aspect of my surroundings, all but my purpose in them. The here and now held a certain—well, that wouldn't interest you."

The leather straps of Odysseus's sandals creaked as he shifted his stance from foot to foot.

"Sit down. It's been a long journey. You should allow yourself to rest."

Odysseus crouched down beside the veil of the man. "There must have been birds. I was busy—intent—"

Teiresias had only to lift up his dead eyes, smooth as quartz, and stare into the man's freshly shocked face.

"Birds!" Odysseus swallowed, rubbing his hands upon his knees. "I saw a gull with a blood-red bill and a yellow band, I remember now. There were many; but, I swear, a certain one of them kept following me."

"Good, now I'll tell you how it's been for me."

"Oh yes," Odysseus answered anxiously, casting his eyes about the growing spectral crowd, for the shades had begun to come into view, to press in upon them there as if to greet one of the newly dead.

"Afterward, Odysseus, I will ask you to tell me what you know," Teiresias said. "Perhaps you, from your vantage point in time, can tell me why I was fated to the life I owned, why I outlived and grieved for all my friends, my lovers and relatives, everyone I ever knew. Why was I, tell me, the one given enough foresight to dwell on what would happen—and without the least power to divert rampaging truths? I want to know. Think what it was to live with that. Tell me—you're alive. You can reason still. Why do you think I alone am here remembering every last gruesome detail even after my own death?"

The two black pinpoints at the centers of the human eyes stared hard at him, perplexed, afraid. I can see the smallest things, the seer thought to himself, staring into the pupils of his visitor unemotionally. My eyes have eyes again. I can see these things. Before him, Odysseus's striped and speckled beard began to shake with terror as the pastel dead with their solemn eyes again began to drift toward them. I can see this living creature as well as I can see these shades, Teiresias said to himself. Perhaps there was something to the blood. He had not meant to drink it, but then, it had smelled rather sweet, like the nectars of fruit, as he remembered them. "Odysseus, you don't know how long I've waited for this. I've the utmost confidence in you. How many people have managed to walk in here alive, think of that. You are extraordinary, an extraordinary man. Tell me what you think."

The shades reached out to touch Odysseus's arm then, and Odysseus fell down, a mortal man on his knees, before Teiresias's seamless robe. "Please," the sailor pleaded, weeping into his own beard where it made a blanket over the dead seer's feet.

"Please— How would I know such things? I might have made mistakes. I see that now. But won't you please help me to get home? We've been beaten, tormented, starved. My men rely on me. I'm breaking down." Beneath his beard the warrior's great square jaw seemed to be made of wood. Teiresias watched it swing back and forth.

"I'll tell you why," Teiresias said to him. "I'll tell you why I've had such a hard time myself. Perhaps you will see reason for sympathy. It's all because of that ridiculous pratfall, that collapse and tumble in the road. I fell once, I struck my head. Life has been unreal ever since. I cannot stop remembering my childhood. Every sound and senseless glimmer brings it back." But the man of war was moaning at his feet. "What's this, Odysseus?" he shouted in alarm. "Stand up, man, for your own sake. Never fall down like that—didn't anyone tell you that? No squirming and sniveling now. You'd like to know the way home."

"If you would only tell me—I would throw myself on the ground and weep with joy."

Teiresias's voice in his disappointment was no bigger than the sound of a hand rubbing nervously at the edge of its sleeve. "You are already on the ground, my only visitor and messenger, and you babble senselessly. Your feet protrude from the mouth of your own grief. Stop now, I will tell you what to do and how to go. But you will have to help me evoke the memories of these shades. Look around you, man. Have you ever seen such a pathetic sight? I had hoped to exchange some thoughts with you. I am alone. Alone with my own thoughts. That's how it is."

The great warrior shook his head again in terror of the dead themselves, and in a vital eagerness. He shrank back from their hands. "You will tell me the way then?"

"I give it to you now, but I will hold you to your promise. We will force the dimness from these parties, if only for the briefest time."

"Please—"

"You will be home soonest if you do not anger the sun by turning your back on it. There is part of your answer—on good faith."

"Part of the answer? I must always sail into the sun? But I would be constantly turning around."

"So it is. Mark well what you turn around. It is your fate. You'll bear with me, I hope. Have hope and faith."

"But, always turning around! What else? Please tell me. Will I never see my dear wife?"

"And your boy. You will see both."

"Teiresias!"

Again a figure came toward them.

"Yes, bring forward your poor mother who, as you know, has been rushing toward you—for something like an eternity— since the moment you first arrived."

Odysseus swallowed hard as if he had a starling in his throat, caught halfway down. "To come here and find her—dead."

"Don't pretend you didn't see her. Go ahead, embrace her. Have some pity here at least. Your father will wait—he is still alive."

In the woods Echo and I sat together handing back and forth a bottle of wine where we would not be found by adults or anyone. We did not cut the wine with water, as was usual, but drank it neat instead. Echo was the only woman among my group of friends; and the fact that we had all accepted her was extraordinary, I realized even then. It was the custom that a woman did not speak with men unless she slept indiscriminately with them, either destined to it as a child or choosing that route herself. Echo had made love to no one, man or woman, in the time that I had known her; and though she was just coming to the age when she would choose her mate, if marriage or love-making were suggested to her, seriously or otherwise, she would not hear of it.

For many reasons I was very fond of Echo. When Echo opened her mouth to speak, one had no need to brace oneself against a complacent note. If one spoke to her seriously, one could be sure that she heard what was said. She had settled quite naturally into what I called not masculine nor feminine but rather her own style. She did not bind her hair up in plaits and braids nor stud it with gold hoopoes. Cut blunt, her hair bounced like a sheaf of yellow wheat between her shoulder blades. I had never in any derisive companies—and I had seen her stand up straight in the face of many—seen self-consciousness among those features I had come to know as my friend's: the tawny wrens of her eyebrows, the amber-fringed brown eyes, the unspectacular ivory sweep of her cheekbones, the slender nose, the full composure of her lips. Echo always wore a tunic as the men did, but she did not leave it a mannish white or neutral hue. Each one of her garments Echo had woven in a saffron fiber, and with them she wore a radically different belt each day. She was unabashed to be seen in the short dresses only the men wore and in the colors women liked. No one had ever seen her breasts—this perhaps enraged the townspeople more than anything else; and I suspected that she had never, even as a little girl, thought seriously about painting them as the other women did to present themselves to the world.

On this particular day I sat with her in the comfortable silence that we often shared. Echo took a drink from the bottle and drew the back of her hand slowly over her mouth. "You would not believe—" she said suddenly.

"What? Finally you've gotten yourself into a fix like the rest of us?" I laughed, then saw that she was disturbed. "What's the matter?"

She looked over her shoulder, through the trees, toward our neighbor's house. I, too, looked to see if I could find what thoughts she had. I could not help peering momentarily for my own troubles, too: the silver sheen of Narcissus's head, the sad temptation of his eyes.

"I thought he was attractive all right," Echo said. "But I couldn't understand—I mean, I was bathing at the spring. That's not so unusual, is it? There was no one there."

My friend Ameinius and I had often gone there ourselves for a swim when we could no longer endure the noise of the others at the gorge where we usually went. I shook my head. I still did not know what man she meant.

"He must have seen me there. He must have known it. Do you know what he did? He stood right there and took off his clothes. He looked at me, took off his clothes, and walked into the water. Teiresias, I—I mean, he's not extraordinary in any way. It was the fact that he did that and looked right at me. It was worse than embarrassing. I was no more significant than space or air."

"But, Echo— You haven't said who it was!" She was rocking herself back and forth, sighing unhappily. She glanced over her shoulder again. "Oh, no," I said. "No, Echo. Not Narcissus."

"It was Graosis," she said. "And then Narcissus did the same. It was as if Graosis was acting as a catalyst for Narcissus. It wasn't who he was. It wasn't even what he looked like. It was what they did."

"Did?"

"The way he looked at me, just like Graosis had, and saw nothing. All my life people have regarded me well. I didn't know I could be so lost. Now I know—"

"Narcissus did nothing?" I asked again, unable to contain my selfishness. I would have felt the same about anyone if Narcissus had been involved. "Not with Graosis, not with you?"

"He looked into my eyes and I wasn't there. Oh—" She tried to smile. "How could someone look at me and see *nothing?*"

"And nothing happened between Narcissus and Graosis?"

Tears sprang out of her eyes. "No, nothing." I was ashamed of myself for being relieved.

"Oh, Echo," I said. "You're not nothing." I took her face between my hands. "I'm sorry it's happened to you, too." I held her close to me until she turned her face up again toward mine.

"I have such an aching, Teiresias. I have such an aching now."

"It's love. It's for the love of a whim we've all lost our minds!"

"No!" She was adamant. "It's not love I feel. I feel nothing now."

"But Echo—" I said.

"Think, Teiresias. Who's asking what I want? Who even cares? The rest of you will go on. I will be like Narcissus's eyes now."

"Oh, Echo—" I said again.

"No, don't say it!" she shouted at me. "Don't say it's because I'm a nymph. That's a stupid thing to say. I'm as smart as any of them, yet no one asks what teacher I want. It's because I am *nothing.* I know that now. That's what I am now—whether I'm a nymph or a girl, or not. It would be the same for you, if you had no teacher. Narcissus only showed me how it was. I am only the prospect of love now, and I don't feel love in me. I only think of him and I know. I can't think of anyone but him. It's not love. The vacancy in his eyes has reflected me now—this is my life and there is nothing here."

It was barely a speck, but it shone out of her face like a coal. "Echo," I said. "Please don't think I'm trying to avoid talking about this. Please don't think that of me. But your lip, Echo?"

Echo jerked away then and her hands flew to her mouth. She pressed her upper lip with her palms.

"It looks like a polished stone, Echo, embedded in your lip. What is it?"

She took her hands away; she ran them through her hair. Her head went down. "I've had it ever since Hera. Hera gave it to me."

"Hera!"

"Of course," she said bitterly. Her hair fell forward. "You didn't think I'd get myself into a simple situation, did you?" She threw her head back against the bark of the olive tree.

I leaned back, too. Hera was known to us for her rage, her unpredictable rage.

"It was glorious," she said, but her terror had twisted any enthusiasm she might have once felt out of her voice. "Take a good look." Her arms went up over her head; the stone shone in her face. "Tomorrow I'll probably be a piece of stinkweed growing beside Narcissus's pond if Hera—or if Zeus—or I'll become one just from my overwhelming obsession with abandonment. He looked right at me, Teiresias, and dropped his clothes. He didn't even care about Graosis. And he cared about me even less. One by one, he dropped his clothes right on top of my feet." She bit her lip. "It's not love we're talking about, Teiresias—it's being frozen out—of significant society."

Hera, Echo told me then, had been doing an unheard-of thing. She had been growing plants in pots on Mount Kithairon. In clumps of soil in a thousand of my teacher Emporous's unfired porridge bowls, the Goddess Hera had been burying seeds. She had taken ten grains from each of the hundred types and declared a top and bottom of each seed. Five of each kind were covered with their more pointed ends up in the bowls, five with them down. I listened cautiously.

"And on the side of the bowl," Echo exclaimed, "she scratches a picture of each plant. You can tell exactly which plant she means! You can see the flower and the fruit! I felt like I could almost have picked it off the side and put it in my mouth," she said. "And that's not all. Beside those, she carves spears with the tip up or down to match the direction of the seed in each bowl. She's so beautiful."

"But, Echo— You mean she's confining seeds to porridge

bowls rather than surrendering them to the ground! She's putting their spirits in pots! For no productive purpose at all?! And she's taken the language of scribes?"

"It's not to *please* herself!" Echo cried. "It's to *learn*. To *prove* that Zeus is no more of a God than she is, or than any of them. God of thunder and rain!" she laughed. "Hera has carried every sprinkling of water for her plants from Athena's spring herself."

"What does Demeter think?"

"She agrees."

No one had ever watered plants themselves as far as I knew. Everyone knew that Zeus was responsible for that. He sent rain in a violent motion through the air to chastise roots, to force them to grow down. Otherwise, everyone knew, the roots would grow up in their need for affection and strangle the leaves. That was understood. "But she already is a God, Echo. She's always been a God—"

"But no less than he! Hera says roots lust after the dead. Plants don't chart their courses by what they would *avoid,* but by what they seek instead! Don't you see? It isn't the wrath of Zeus driving them down; it's what they themselves prefer. Water does not have to come directly out of the sky for a plant to grow; it can be brought in other ways. By Hera, by other Gods. By people themselves." Echo shook back her hair just as I was doing the same. "Think of it. It means no drought." Awkwardly we laughed as two people often do when they begin to see eye to eye.

"You've seen what she looks like when she's angry, when she goes through town looking for him—her face in wild contortions, her hands clawing at that hair. Up close that hair represents every color a head has ever carried on it—human, bird, or animal: even the reds, greens, and violets, the black and gold. Her braids came tumbling down in front of me, Teiresias. 'Miracles!' she laughed at me. I didn't know what to say to her. After all, I'm just me. She threw open the window onto the courtyard—"

"You've been there then!" I exclaimed.

She held up her hand. "All the other Gods but Zeus were there. According to Hera, he's never where he's supposed to be. 'When it comes to me and mine,' Hera whispered to me, 'that big Zero will have nothing to say about growth!' And the other Gods looked up at us. They applauded! They beat the table with their fists. Apollo threw the thigh of an ox against the wall. 'Another vote for sanity,' he cried. 'Throw the bum out! Strike down his name!' Can you believe it? They want to get rid of him," Echo said to me. "Can you believe the way they said all of that and said it in front of me?"

On her thin legs her beige hairs rose up at the thought. "Every week she sends someone to get me, Teiresias. You should see the way the rainbow of her hair floats around my shoulder; you should see how kind she is to me. She's nothing like what everybody says she is. And I've helped her, Teiresias. I really have."

"But now it's Narcissus?" I asked. "Now you're in love with him? Now all you're interested in is him?"

"Now—now I'm a fool. I'm the biggest fool in the world. I'm just like everybody else. I can't think anymore. What makes me want him, Teiresias? What makes me the way I am?" I shook my head as her tears flowed down.

I wondered at how Hera had blasphemed herself and all the Gods—especially Zeus, my own father's father. It was true that in her youth my grandmother had been poking with a stick at a bundle of laundry on a rock, leaning over, when she felt a raindrop strike her back. She had felt it grow large and cumbersome, the arms wrapping around her waist as a great gust of wind blew her skirts up over her head. It was then, she had said, that she felt the penetrating moisture of rain between her legs. Perhaps it hadn't been Zeus at all, I thought.

Perhaps nothing was as we thought it to be. Here was my teacher Emporous sending pots, which I had helped to make, to Kithairon for Hera's experiments when I thought they were meant for Troy. I leaned back and took up the wine; I offered it to Echo. Hairs grew only in an upward direction as far as I knew. I wondered if somewhere beneath Echo's skin and my own, too, there might be rows of tiny seeds planted every which way and beneath them millions of determined fibers that slowly dug their way toward the Underworld they desired. I also wondered whether if we as children could grow to be adolescents and then adults, then the same might not be true of the world. Might the world, too, not grow old and die?

Zeus had gained his entrance by trickery. There was no doubt about it—at first. Too many people had seen the bird clowning and flirting in front of her, falling in a pathetic feint at her feet. When the Great Goddess Hera finally held him to her sympathetic breast and stroked the cuckoo's head, he resumed his form. The God of thunder would not let go of her for three hundred years. And for three hundred years all the world and all the other Gods looked on at the trembling confusion of their legs. At first, the people noted the horrible undulations, the terrified shrieks with fear, with abhorrence, and then disgust. And then, with the procession of generation after generation by that site where the naked limbs of Gods were casting lewdly about, the common feeling of revulsion in the people turned to one of embarrassment—as all futile resentments will—until eventually her defilement and his malefaction were a joke to them. The comedy poured from town to town, ravishing the tenderness of little children, rasping the sensitivities of men and women all across the countryside. They became small copies of the joke themselves, in jest, until finally during one long season—no one remembers which, whether hot or cold, wet or parched—the Goddess rarely cried or fought her brother anymore, and those who had heard the beginning for themselves had been transported to the Underworld in funeral urns thirteen or fourteen generations before. The Gods' grunts and sighs had become a little like the wind heard frequently on a windy hill. People looked up from their supper bowls and said,

"Windy night." They went on sopping juices with their bread. Hera had lost her authority, her self-esteem, and most of her generosity, too. As all sound people do when tortured for long periods of time—and Gods do the same—she had changed. She looked for hope in the lot that now was hers, though she did not hope that it could ever be what it once had been. And the people? They had over the centuries incorporated the joke into their lives—the women emulating the fallen Hera with sighs and shrieks, the men riding a coarse gesture into the ground.

And that was how it happened that we who lived at that time had no insight into who we were and had been or who Hera really was. An atrocity had been committed, and nothing was done when the rape was new. It went on until it seemed incontrovertible, and therefore a natural way of life—for all concerned. That is the way all peoples, in groups or individually, may be worn away, oppressed. We heard the name of Zeus and we fell in reverence to our knees. All of this I heard in astonishment from Echo who had heard it from the Gods and who whispered it to me as adolescents will.

I prepared myself as if for my own wedding feast. Steaming cauldrons of water were brought to my bath by the maids and then in the greatest solemnity I was bathed, my nails were pared and rubbed with stones, my body oiled and toweled, my hair brushed until it hung like a black and shining wave. The maids were dismissed, and I put on my finest linen tunic and fastened my one gold girdle at my waist. I then took up the small comb to straighten the new hairs sprouting from my chin. I was already looking forward to the moment when they would be ceremoniously shaved, when I would be considered an adult. Two bracelets I had buttoned around each arm; and, as I passed the glass windows along our street, I did not recognize the young man who had grown large in those panes. My shoulders were wider than they had been that morning surely, my arms thicker than I had known. I was as tall as most men in town, though not gigantic as the Mykenaens were. I had a clear face and my teeth were still good.

There then on the approach to the palace my assurance was suddenly checked. My friend Ameinius was crouched beside the road. "Ameinius—Ameinius—" I said, but I could not think which words of consolation should come next. Around his bent neck my friend Ameinius had slung the testicles of a wild ass like an immense pouch. At the sight of me, Ameinius sprang up and grabbed my arm. There, too, against his cheek, on a silver chain, shivered the skeleton of a chicken; there rattled the stone teeth of horse, mole, and hyena; there slithered against his skin the tongue of a dead chameleon.

"See how it beats?" Ameinius gasped, pointing to a serpent's bloody heart. "And that's not all—" He did not go on. I could see that the heart did not beat, that indeed that was not all. A belt passed over one of Ameinius's bare broad shoulders, across his chest, and under the opposite arm; and on it were sewn hundreds of tiny ampules, each, I supposed, another of his amulets. Owl's gizzard, rat's ears and liver, raven's excrement. I could not see beyond the rage that flew up in me. Dog's gall, goat's brain, wasp's wings, wolf's flesh, fat, head. He wore a loincloth the likes of which had not been seen since Knossos. On the front of the apron he had pinned a braided circle of human hair.

"These are not the old times!" I cried. "We are not country fanatics who go off and shave our heads and spirit away the evil eye! Ameinius!"

"We'll see if Narcissus puts his evil eye on me," Ameinius said, looking toward the gate. His eyes were glazed, his voice as flat as a stillborn lake. "We'll see if he spirits my teacher away."

Here now we approached the gate by way of the inclined road, late, I with my fears locked in, Ameinius with them hanging about his person fore and aft. The grade was steep, the evening heat unbearable. As we passed through the entrance, a husk of bread hurtled down from the tower and struck Ameinius on the arm.

"Will you look at this! Look at this, I say!" Ameinius cried. "I have been pierced by the guards. They've all agreed. It's the king's decree."

"That's right," I laughed. "Breaded to death. And everyone is in on it."

"It's a sign," he shouted, "of things to come. Think of his invitation. Do you call those friendly words?"

"Polydoros is just stretching his limbs. He says what he sees. And how could that offend?" I laughed in Polydoros's absence and then softened at the thought of him awkward on his young throne, soon to rule from the grave. "No one can see a man so clearly as Polydoros and still appreciate him. As for this crumb from the guards, Ameinius—"

"From the guards? Gods! From the Gods, I say!"

"Ameinius, leave room for accident, won't you? Or for jest."

Ameinius was rubbing his arm peevishly. "He has no right to embarrass me. To turn everyone against me. As if I hadn't had enough—"

"It's lucky you weren't hit somewhere else," I said. "Skewered by a husk in your trembling balls." I pointed at the great furred sack he wore around his chest.

"It isn't funny," he said. "It's not hilarious at all."

"Or in your gizzard," I said, poking at his ribs.

"Narcissus will probably choose tonight!"

"Or on your lovely little lavender tongue." With my fingernail I flicked the tiny piece of flesh on its chain next to all the rest.

"You want him, too! Emporous or not—you can't deny you want him."

It was true. I could not deny it. Forever, I thought, with no reprieve. To Ameinius I said nothing. We had passed the tower, and the two massive doors swung shut behind us. I turned to watch the giants straining to lift the metal crossbar into place. The doors were bolted, tied, and knotted, the cables wound again and again. The two men sank down, their tremendous backs a small but further buttress. If we had been the enemy we would never have gotten this far. We would have been assailed on the ascending ramp by spears from the tower, not by bread. We would have been unguarded on that side, our shields in our left hands.

Three years before, Ameinius and I had gone to celebrate at the river for our yearly first swim. Naked, the other boys were throwing themselves off cliffs to enter feet first where the river pooled into deep waters. A long papyrus rope swung like a leg from a tree, and on this, back and forth, Ameinius and I swung together, chest to chest, face to face, new hair to new hair, clenched in a knot.

"What is our understanding then?" Ameinius asked as the cliffs, the water, and the delicate shoulders of the younger boys reeled above and below us, around and around. "Perhaps we should drown him."

I laughed, having been irritated by our mutual friend to such an extent that I, too, had imagined this.

Ameinius said, "Have you seen the way he swings himself in front of me? Then he accuses me as if I had crept up on him! Have you seen those spider fingers of his, winding their way through my hair?"

I gave a push with one foot against the ledge and we swung out again. I nodded into my friend's face, for Narcissus had also provoked me and then shoved me physically aside. "Have you settled in with the old man yet?" I asked, for Ameinius was supposed to have found a teacher high among the king's counselors.

"That's all bunk," he said bitterly. "I'm to be the only unplucked flower in Thebes."

"What's that?" I asked. I had been about to turn our conversation toward new alliances. I had been about to speak of my internship with Emporous, about what a relief it had been to me, the small irritations I felt, the nervousness and excitement of approaching rites. All of these—or the ease to speak of them—had been squelched in the face of Ameinius's disconcerted state. It was as if, in soaring out on the rope and back again, all that had been good had turned on itself.

Ameinius thrust out his leg and hurled us viciously away from the cliff. "In spite of how I feel about Narcissus, I could have loved Graosis. Since I was nine—for five whole years!—everyone has known that he would take me as his favorite, they've called me Graosis's vine. Now it's all gone. Take one guess upon whom the wise man's eyes are dithering. Take one guess."

"Narcissus?" I weakly asked. I could almost see that one misplaced eye flying up to flirt in the counselor's face.

"Who else? Who else?" Ameinius cried, the muscles of his arms bunched up beside the rope. "Narcissus has the loveliest shoulders in all of Greece; and once the old man loved me, once he did." Ameinius began to weep. "I'm the laughingstock for everyone, and all because of him."

"Perhaps you should take a girl and forget about being an apprentice. Leap ahead of us all?"

"What?" Ameinius wept. "And be laughed at for that, too?" What he said was true, I knew that. We swung back and forth.

For a brief time after Hera resigned herself to Zeus, she'd tried to retain her self-esteem by saying, Yes, oh yes, this is what I want—for Zeus was what she had. For a brief time even Hera failed to notice that he no longer heard her speak. Zeus could not see her authority without worrying about himself. I love you, Zeus her brother said.

In the silence Hera could still offer the spontaneous thought, the spontaneous smile without thinking of the corrections that would follow, the long analysis and speeches Zeus would concoct if by chance he'd caught a phrase. She put aside the realization that she had given in to him in more ways than one, that now—having done the first against her will—now when she reached for him he grasped her wrists and turned her quietly but firmly away. In better and distorted memories she could bury the fact that when he reached toward her in affection it was only after he had seen a rain of sorrow on her face. How it brought out his tenderness!

It was in a moment of frustration that she presented him with her new agricultural plan, the plan that would make him more a part of the whole than the entire source he had become. And Zeus, caught as if for the first time in hearing her, said that he could not remember how long it had been since he had heard an intelligent word come out of her blank mouth. He wished he had heard one now. No droughts, he laughed. There it was—shining undeniably before him—a threat, though she swore it didn't have to be, that they could all live together and share what they as Gods controlled. And the other Gods agreed. He could relax a little more.

"Could it be?" he stammered. She had frightened him with her very presence then. His own inadequacy swelled in him. Share?! he thought. Share?! And for the first time in his existence, no words would come to him. She waited for what she had come to expect: the storm of words that would go on and on at a tangent to what she had said, that would avoid taking her thoughts into account. But there was not one sound in him to break the vast expanse that filled them both up. He merely blinked.

He had been seeking the one long-lasting devotion, he told himself, the one calm movement with another that would never take him by surprise. He'd thought he had found it in her. But now she had frightened him, and that monologue, which had been his medium, his sure defense, had broken down. They looked at one another as if for the first time and could not believe how vacuous the air had become. "Ah!" he cried out then, seizing on the subject of rain. "Why yes! Why yes!" The stream flowed from his mouth, and it had nothing at all to do with her or what she'd said about damming up rivers and making lakes.

"What's wrong?" Zeus called, following after her quickly retreating form, for he could not stand to be rejected any more than he could stand to recognize others. Both called his attention to someone else. "What is wrong with you?" he said. He reached out then, thinking he saw in her a discomfort that he had just conquered himself: loss of words. He saw himself in her and his empathy soared as it had never done before. But she would not be touched.

He reaches for me only when I'm sad! she thought. I will not be touched *only* when I'm weak.

"I touch you. You turn away!" he cried. "I will have affection from my wife! I will have understanding!"

"But you only touch me when I cry—"

"I touch," he repeated. "I touch—you turn away. Of course, you cry! Hera!" he said. And then he said something Hera could not believe she'd heard him say. "Hera!" he said. "You never listen to me!"

He would go somewhere else, he declared. *Somewhere. Someone.* But he had been somewhere else all along. Burying himself between the legs of women who talked as Hera had at first, he attempted to punish them both and everyone concerned. Conversation, love, rose from his lovers' lips; and he listened because he did not know them. They were still images, projections of what he himself could imagine them to be. These experiences he brought home and remembered aloud until Hera could not contain herself. She spoke in a way that she had never heard herself speak; and he listened—enough to say, I will not hear this.

Hera knew it now: Zeus could not construct anything with anyone. Each day for him had to be a starting over again with himself at the center. He had all the wisdom and only the wisdom that beginnings can give. He was the compass with only one leg.

One by one his new passions, as he called them (for he loved the women passionately), turned, sighed, wept, stammered, became inarticulate and small. Why were they all alike? he asked himself. Why could he find no one? Anything! He would do anything for a momentary release from his loneliness. A worm was not too base a thing for him to become, his soul immediately at rest beneath the tight restrictions of a slick and silvery skin. He burrowed in, looking for that thing he hoped, believed, and knew to be residing in this world where he had, he knew, no insignificant amount of control. He sought one thing. He called it contentment, a transformation in his life. He sought *cocoon*. He would become a dumb animal if he must for the sake of this; he would jeopardize the equilibrium of any and all for his momentary release from the distress he felt at being alive in his own skin. And why not? he asked himself—with the wife he loved grown brittle and mean, her voice a mere stammering. She had become strange to him, dependent, repugnant. She had become nothing at all like herself.

All of this Hera had understood. And Hera had told it to Echo. What are the roots of subjugation, humiliation, of madness, too? It can be seen more clearly in those children, Hera said, to whom no one has listened in their small lives, in those children who speak quite clearly and their parents reply always to something else, to what they have expected or wanted to hear. What is it to lose one's confidence, one's sexuality, one's intelligence, one's voice and power to act independently? What is it for a mortal, for a God? It is much the same.

Once, the Goddess had said to herself—for when the present is bad, always the past seems good—once there had been a better moment that had seemed to last three hundred years. There must have been. Once there was a flood of recognition between two souls. Where had his dark eyes gone, the eyes that followed her everywhere and sent his gaze deep into and through her own bright, comprehending pupils into the swallowing at the back of her throat? Even that degradation now seemed better to her than what she was now. Here was Zeus doing a little two-step in the compensation of her memory; there he was humming fanfare and accompaniment to her tears. Now she cried alone.

Why did she not leave him? Hera asked herself, as frequently as Apollo and the others asked it. I will leave him *now*, Hera said to herself. Now I will leave and then he will be gone and who will hum a fanfare to my tears? Who will build his ragged life around my bones? She could not move in any direction now without faulting herself. Surely there was something she might have done, might still do. I have grown ugly, she said. Ugly and stupid, Hera said, not seeing the others as they gazed up, in full knowledge of her, from their conferences in the courtyard. How does one who is not oneself leave what one has begun? How does one finish anything? Her rage rose up in her and excoriated all questioning. She would destroy those he turned to, those who came between herself and her hope. Hera had become not unlike the trickster Zeus.

Yet there came a relief into Hera's existence for a time. There was Echo, who would listen as well as speak, whose voice was clear as a perfect bell in the Olympian air, who could discern and say quietly, Don't you see, Hera, how this all occurred? This is the way of your past. There was a moment here and there when Hera again felt herself to be whole, and that was when she heard the lilting, rational, strong voice of intelligence. Echo stroked the hair back from Hera's neglected forehead. Echo said, You have words worth saying, Hera. Do you know that?

Hera strides the snow; she thinks of Zeus. She laughs. She is waiting for someone else. Her attendants are following in her wake at a respectful distance, a distance learned through repetition of wrath. She turns and smiles at them. They titter nervously. The color has risen in her cheeks. "Oh, come on," she says. "I won't bite." They titter nervously. "Today I won't." They rush toward her—perhaps it is again the time when she was kind, the time before they stood helpless as sheep among other sheep and watched her brother rip each seam. Tomorrow the witty little mortal will come; perhaps that is what makes

Hera smile today. Long white coat, white cap of fur, muff, the color in her cheeks that is like no color they have ever seen, even in her prismatic hair.

"Tomorrow the young lady will be here again?" the bravest one asks. The Goddess smiles. She looks down the white crags and slopes into the scrub pines at the tree line, into the laden conifers and far below into the oaks and beeches that have gone green in the valley of spring. Even the trees wilt for lack of rain. It is through all this that Echo will travel tomorrow to be with her.

Tonight Hera will stretch her legs into that glorious emptiness where Zeus in his infidelity is not, will not be, and think of other times: Echo beside her, quietly watching the morning light pouring through the even tenor of a life they are making, that they believe in enough to build; Echo with her strong thighs and taut calves on Kithairon, pacing off the rocky ground, stooping to set down firmly the painted stones at the perimeters where the glass house—which Echo in her ingenuity has designed—will hold Hera's plants and protect them from sudden rain; Echo in the courtyard in the company of Gods, her elbows on the table, speaking awkwardly at first, and then in confidence, making suggestions about the reconstruction of the world; Echo's arm stretched unflinchingly around her shoulders as Zeus walks through oblivious; the applause of Gods.

When the morning stretches its white light through the blue window glass, Hera is up and calling for her bath. Seven attendants are bathing her on the day when Echo will arrive. The long hair is combed, washed, combed again in the array that falls nearly to her feet. The hair is braided, then wrapped round and round her head. When the maids are finished with this ritual bath, the hair will be brushed out full again to fall in waves. Hot water pours into the pool, the back is lathered, the small figure—with powers for and against all things but one—is scrubbed as the women lean down over the mosaic tiles. Today Zeus is of no concern to anyone. Hera throws the sponge at the wall and laughs. It sticks there like a cork at the center of the fresco's mouth. Today a small woman with a beige stride and penetrating smile will show Hera again what it is to think for herself. "Get in, get in," Hera calls to her maids. Today Hera will be herself. In that chamber they titter in around her, splashing up a name. Her own. But Echo has forgotten. She has gone somewhere else instead.

Could the old man at the door to the megaron have protested more? Could he have said more against the appearance of Ameinius by shouting and thrusting weapons than with his cold, implacable gaze, his hand out: a shaft between us and the salubrious voices on the far side of the wall. Discreetly he eyed donkey balls, loincloth, coxcomb, chicken bones. "I will have to inquire," he said.

"You will have to inquire?" Ameinius asked, incredulous.

The arm did not move out of the way. "Perhaps I do not recognize you. I will ask the king."

"You will have to inquire?!" Ameinius cried out again. "I am Ameinius! That Ameinius who was called the old friend, the good friend, of Polydoros. I've been here a thousand times!."

The attendant tapped the door and stepped inside. "You will find me here!" Ameinius shouted. "I will not have moved to left or right! I will not have batted a lash."

"Ameinius," I asked, "must you?"

The door fell open, and I heard our names announced in the voice of an embarrassed old man. His past, a reservation in the dignity of his mouth, was to me a relief. Ameinius rattled in, the ass's balls and all his other paraphernalia flopping against his chest.

I crept in after him, making directly for the couch where Emporous lay propped up on his left elbow, dipping his right hand into the foods as they were set on the small table in front of him. I lowered myself into my place beside him. "You would not believe," I said.

"I see," he said. "I believe."

At the center of the room near the hearth, Ameinius flapped about, looking through the utter silence toward paired couch after paired couch, toward the two flimsy tables that had been shoved together to accommodate the rarest guests. There the ladies sat, Echo with them, on chairs, uncomfortable, and silent as they were instructed to be. Near the king's chair, on the king's couch, reclined Polydoros, staring at Ameinius's approach, and beside him lay the honored Narcissus, who went on tearing bread between his hands. "Ameinius seeks his place," called out Ameinius, who stood directly before them. "Ameinius seeks his place, I say! Narcissus! I seek my place with you—" A flush of anger had gone up into the men's faces at the sight of him. Narcissus did not glance up from the food he held in his hand, and the king's face was implacable.

"Here it is," the meekest voice repined from the far side of the room. In the corner, a tangle of hair was moved aside; and the once-humble Ameinius clattered toward him in angered confusion, readjusted himself, and threw himself down next to Nesos, glancing furiously all around.

Emporous bent near me, but Ameinius was shouting again. Emporous raised his brow, adjusted the cushions at his back, and rested his head. I lay back and sighed, too. In this company it was Ameinius, Echo, Nesos the Island, Polydoros, and Emporous whom I had loved since childhood, and in a different way, it was Narcissus, too. An overwhelming sadness crept over me.

"Perhaps we should have a game of cottabus right now," King Polydoros abruptly said. Polydoros stroked Narcissus's thigh. "Perhaps we should know this once and for all, what do you say? We will play a game of cottabus. And the winner will have Narcissus for himself. All the men will play."

At this decree, Narcissus's hand clutched his own wrist, and I saw his mother and mine gasp. Echo, too, for another reason, went completely white. "Only the men?" I saw her lips say. "Polydoros, it isn't right," she mouthed. "It isn't right. And what about Narcissus?"

But the clamoring had already begun for the first try at throwing the wine. "Narcissus! Narcissus!" All the older men and many of the younger ones were crying out that the metal stand be brought, that we commence immediately in the sport. For all of them now had a chance. Narcissus showed no sign of emotion.

"This is not a good idea," I shouted out as loudly as I could. "This is not fair to Narcissus. Or to anyone."

"Narcissus must choose for himself!"

"I have decided," Polydoros said.

"How can Polydoros do this?" I whispered.

Emporous touched my arm, and I saw his look of apprehension.

"The Gods will tell us," someone called. "Just as the king has said, the Gods will answer it in the game."

"Yes, yes! I agree. The Gods will answer it," Ameinius yelled. "I will go first!" Unbidden, his limbs lurched toward the center of the room. Silence fell over the hall again at the sight of him. And then he began to speak out, more to himself than to anyone in his desperate, shaken voice. "I will have it over with," Ameinius quavered, "and if the sound is good—and how could it be inferior, how could everything go wrong for me? I mean, how could the Gods— No! The sound will be good, clear, pure! A sign of my life, of the trust Narcissus has in me but is afraid to show. You will forgive me then, will you not?" he said to all of us. "You will forgive me when I have won him? When he knows himself? You won't hold it against me? No, you will let me pass, with him. With Narcissus, my friend. I have been so long in the sadness of this—I hardly know from day to day— I mean . . . Bring the stand! Won't you, please?"

The servant was called to pace the distance then, and Ameinius was told where to stand on the tiled floor. The brass disc was set up and the wine poured in Ameinius's cup to the rim. Quietly we each took a sip out of our own and sang out a note for the Gods to speak truly in the tone.

"I would have someone," Ameinius said, holding the cup

tightly to his laden chest with both hands and closing his eyes. "I would be a friend to him, a lover, a brother, a father, a son. I would hold someone if he would hold me. If it is the Gods' will, I would have him love me, too. Narcissus—" His arm swept up and the wine flew toward the disc. Through the air it sailed: past the white tunics of all the men who waited there, past the stationary colors at the two square tables where the women sat, between the pillars at the end of the hall. Secretly we each hoped that he would lose; and we, those of us who had known him for so long, hoped that he would hear, for his sake, the clear tone of Narcissus's assent in the song of the Gods. I saw him imagining it himself as the liquid struck the brass. He stood there stunned, listening.

No one said a word as the cymbal rang out with a cry of tin in a false, wavering tone. It offended the ear, and crept along the spine long after its impact. Stiffly Ameinius walked to his couch, flinging off parts of animals as he went. He lay down in tears, and flung back his arms behind his head. Graosis, his old teacher, stared after him. Toward the vaulted ceiling Ameinius cried then uncontrollably, his sobs echoing like a child's throughout the room. Even Dykastes turned toward the wall and coughed in pity.

"Ameinius!" I cried out, seeing him like that. I rose up to go to him, but Emporous put out his hand again. Ameinius once again lunged toward the center of the hall.

Ameinius has plucked up the bills of geese from his errant costume, thrusting them over his hands. On the one hand, an orange beak; on the other, a beak of flamelike fire. Together he clapped them, clacking across the floor in his dance. For a moment I did not know whether or not he had recovered. In the loincloth back and forth Ameinius threw his hips. Fingers and thumbs worked his castanets. The circle of human hair flapped up, flapped down on his body. Then beaks were in Graosis's hair. And then Ameinius had drunkenly struck at the old man. Narcissus's arms went up over his head, and Graosis shoved him into the center of the floor again.

"I will throw the wine again!"

Ameinius has flung the wine again. It hits with a humiliating clang. He throws yet again. Again he throws it hysterically, and he has slumped down. He knows it now: Narcissus will be with somebody else. Someone, not Ameinius. Narcissus will never touch the weak and yearning body of the bright, forlorn, lost, and necessary Ameinius.

"It is clear," the king said, looking at Narcissus huddled for comfort in Graosis's arms. "It is clear, finally, whom Narcissus would choose. This is the end of the game. Ameinius, please sit down." But Ameinius could no more make it back to Nesos's side than he could win Narcissus. Who could stop his hideous inhuman wailing? Around and around the room it reverberated.

A young woman crouched now, in tears herself, before Ameinius. And beside Echo, another one: my mother, speaking as no woman had spoken in the hall before. "Look, Ameinius," she said softly. "Can you look at this? You see on this vase a picture of two things, Ameinius." She held the receptacle toward him. "What are they? Tell me now." She lay one hand on his back.

"A *hippopotamos*," he sobbed. We all watched her hand moving up and down over his spine. "Two inches tall," he sobbed again.

"And what else?" she asked. She put her palm on his dripping brow. "What else, Ameinius? There's a good boy. Be calm now."

"A man," he cried. "There is a man!"

"And how tall is a man?" she asked; her eyes, too, were red. He looked at my mother then, a long time. He was not crying now. "How tall is a man?"

Dazed, he looked at the vase. "You see, Ameinius," she said, looking into his eyes. "Can you see me?"

"Yes," he said.

"We see here a picture of the *hippopotamos*, nearly as tall as the man and far wider. In life, it is wider than him, wider than a horse or a bull." She stroked his brow. "These things today are

86

as small as a picture. We've all fallen in love with Narcissus. He seems very large to us today. But soon he will be just a picture. All of us are losing him. Are we all nothing now? Can we be nothing now, just because of this? There are so many good things."

"Yes, Ameinius," someone said hopefully. "We are all still together. We have all of us lost him now, except Graosis."

Ameinius looked at the vase. And Narcissus on his birthday wrapped his arms around his legs and buried his face in his knees. Graosis had tenderly placed his arm around his unfeeling shoulders.

Ameinius's mouth dropped open then, and his bared chest heaved as if he could not get the words to come out. For a long time we waited, but he put both of his hands over his face then.

"Do we have to be nothing now?" my mother said. "Just because of what has happened here? Can you hear what I say? We will show you some good things." Beside them Echo slumped, unnoticed, listening, too, merely a lump in the throat of her own life now. Ameinius's pain was the room now, in which for a moment we lived, interrupted only by the fire, the brilliant stone stars laid into the floors by slaves who would never tread upon them freely. The massive stone pillars rose up above his unrelenting misery. How long had he known it? How many years had he waited?

"I've lost Narcissus! And Ameinius, where is Ameinius now?" He cried at the side of the urn. "Hippopotamoose! Hippopotamoose! Where is Ameinius? I am two . . . two . . . inches tall!" His eyes were completely glazed, and he had begun to shake again. "Hippopotamoose," he whimpered. Then, abruptly, he went silent as the jar he held. Like the man painted beside the animal there, he stared directly into the small and spiraled ear; and there in the ear of the beast he had never in life seen, wandering in the imagination of what he had become, his mind was lost to everyone. My mother knelt beside him, stunned. Finally she turned.

"Did you know I mentioned your name to Hera, Narcissus?"

Echo whispered in a lost voice. In a Goddess, ichor flows. Soon Echo will be a shadow in this room, a repetition of voices not her own.

"Maybe I've done the wrong thing," my mother said, bewildered and hopeless.

"No," Polydoros said. "You didn't. We will do something," he said. "Sit down. We will restore Ameinius to us somehow."

Polydoros stood a long moment looking at what could be seen of his old friend, and then he sat down alone on his throne. We all sat down. He took a slice of fruit and put it in his mouth. He chewed slowly, looking on at Ameinius and Nesos who had come to him. "Something else is troubling me," he said. "I feel it important to know these things now, before we go on. Teiresias," he said unexpectedly. Everyone turned toward me. "Tell us what you know."

"Know?!" I screeched, sitting bolt upright.

"Yes. You must tell us what you know of Ameinius's chances. And then you must tell us what you know of Mykenos's plans against us now that Edus is gone. Will they attack Thebes? Will there be a war soon?"

"Know? I know nothing at all."

"Stop," Polydoros said in a voice that was his as king and that had never been his as friend. "If you can know the future, then isn't it only right that you give us, your friends, the benefit? On the one matter, we must know our own friend's fate. On the other, it's your duty to tell us. Go on with it."

"I tell you," I cried out, "I had no idea, I mean I have no understanding of what has happened to Ameinius. He is in love with Narcissus just like everyone else."

But I had already seen him in that moment laid out in his funeral urn. I looked over to where Narcissus was huddled in a similar fashion, unfeeling against the side of the old man. "And," I said angrily, "I know nothing of your Mykenaeans! Why don't you ask Basilieus, your advisor in these things? Ask Dykastes. Why ask me when I've only once been out of Thebes, and then I was such an infant I didn't know what I saw.

Why—" I leaped off the couch. "How can you ask me?" I struck my chest. "Ask the Juryman, I say. Ask anyone, ask Dykastes, who would make a fool of me when I speak. No one believes in me here."

Emporous reached out and laid his hand on my back. "What is it?" I shouted, shaking him off. "I know nothing, I tell you. I am not responsible for what goes on here. Did I put Narcissus up like a calf in a lottery? Do we sell our friends in a game here? These are not human ways, you have lost all human ways. Did I do this? Did I say that tomorrow the Mykenaeans will storm your gate and slaughter all the goats in the outer court? Did I tell you tomorrow Athena will squat down on our roof and call for war? Why don't you ask my mother? She's Athena's nymph. But she won't know any more than what I tell you now. As if you didn't already know everything. Why would you ask me to deliver you? Can't you see it for yourselves— In one hundred and fifty years Thebes will be a pockmark on this land. Not one man living on this spot will remember grandeur when the name of Thebes is said, and it will be you and yours who drag it down!"

The heat broke out on my brow. I was going to be ill, I knew, for what I'd said was true. How I knew it I didn't know. And the sweat poured down. I rushed toward the door, and just as quickly Emporous followed after me. "He's very ill. I'm sorry, I apologize," he blurted out. "He has overexerted himself in the feast. Excuse us, please." Out the corner of my eye, I saw my mother stricken helpless by all these things.

"I will take him home," Emporous said. "There is little use in questioning. He is upset at what has happened to Ameinius here." He led me out past the trembling little man.

But it was of my friends I dreamed.

Emporous wraps the young Teiresias in blankets and skins. He stirs up the fire on the hearth and sets him near it. Back and forth he rushes to make hot drinks; he covers him.

But Teiresias is chattering. He is everywhere at once, his body fighting to contain it all: the party where Teiresias is not, but thinks he is, the room in which he sits but cannot see. Now Echo is a hollow, unearthly voice in the weird cubicle of his imaginings: Echo will never again be touched or loved or seen. Today, tomorrow, yesterday are trapped beneath his one pale skin. Further pain grips him in his entrails as, somewhere, he knows now, his other two childhood friends are wrapped together around a piece of earth, one a speck in water, one in dirt. The room sways back and forth, as if the walls will all fall down, while a deep sweat breaks in waves over his brow and crown. Over the basin in the floor he crouches. Beside him, Emporous, too, is hunkered, unfelt, unseen, as if unknown, staring into the pale green slime his young friend has produced.

Then, out of the darkness of Teiresias's mind, a small red object flies, flung along an endless filament, and beside it a cone like a dead gray sky.

This Teiresias cannot accept. He feels it in his wretched gut and knows only this. This gray specter is no bird, yet it flies where it must not fly. This has become his purpose now, no matter how long his life.

Emporous sits back. There, lying on the tiles of the central floor, in Teiresias's vomitus, is a silver-gray fish—still mouthing air.

Polydoros has already sent for the *hippopotamos* Ameinius thought himself to be: a lesson in perspective for those who would be obsessed with those who see nothing but themselves.

"I know nothing of Mykenos. How can I know Mykenos when I have never seen the place?"

One hundred slaves bear one hundred white moths to set

loose in the hall. The megaron has never seemed so small, so large. The colored tiles of the floor no longer seem a game. The frescoes loom up toward the ceiling vault, the pillars and the plastered beams. The pairs of men and the huddle of women are obscured by them. Silence rises like an acknowledgment from throat to throat. Thebes is still as a land smitten by snow. Only a slight breathing of wings can disturb Thebes now. The king's head is resting in his hands; soon the slaves will stir them up again. Everywhere, everything is white now.

This is not a moment for thought or words. Soon life will move on again; soon memory will no longer know what was imagined in this room, what was real. Perhaps the slaves will feel their power, and be steadied in their course. In a single motion perhaps, they will make a motion in the world. Even they do not know how the moment is chosen, how they will suddenly act in unison, how they will rise from the places where they've crouched waiting to rise up to complete the ritual. Silently their tongues fly about in their mouths until a momentum reaches knees and feet.

And up! they have flown about the room, stirring the delicately winged and captive things until closer and closer they circle to the central fire, a whirling of white petals, white cloth. Thebes looks up. There is a new pillar in front of Polydoros, King, feathered in a cone up to the roof where the fire has been smothered.

Alone, Ameinius imagines himself outside Narcissus's door. Alone, hideously sanctified, the bearer of an impure note, he is rattling in his bones. He has already thrown the wine: it goes home, as he does. How can they have left him alone? How can Narcissus be sitting on Graosis's lap? He hears them laughing at him.

Narcissus's mother is the first to find the boy. It is a moment so grotesque she feels as if she, Blue Leiriope, were struck in the head. Doublet of swords. She has yet to find her own son—little, pert, unattainable one, admired by all, grown rigid as a hedge among underwater fronds along the border of his own enforced immaturity.

Leiriope moves away from the door most oddly, jerking from room to room, bearing the image of what even now is perched, strange bird, on her front step: the dead naked boy, Ameinius. A pair of swords runs through his smooth finely haired abdomen and out again: bloody, tinged green, carrying a tatter of kidney on one of the bronze blades.

Perhaps it is not true? Leiriope flings the door open again. The sun comes up across the courtyard, so blushing, nearly purple across the stone, up to this marble boy's white lips.

Narcissus is nowhere to be found; the maids are elsewhere, already looking for him.

Emporous made the funeral urn, a meter tall, spinning it with nimble hands, and then he cut it: still damp, with the knife, opened it like a gourd. On the perfectly smooth interior, he painted your best friend's face so that your friend would not be afraid. And on the outside: the glaze over iron-rich clay, highly refined, mixed with water. He painted on it the pictures of your loved one's life. The lost Ameinius will live here now, wrapping his arms around stiff legs; he will rest a cheek on one knee as once was done so long ago in his mother's womb, so recently. And on the outside of this urn, we will live, painting in the early morning hours, carrying pots and holding up the brushes large and small.

Here are the cenotaphs along the way, a stone sema each to stand for Narcissus and Echo. Her body goes unfound, his unretrieved. Narcissus is said to have heard her voice, lithe Echo's lilting tones, calling to him even as he was in the water. No one can retrieve him from such depths, not his would-be lovers, not his mother. Not even Chariklo can wade in deeper and deeper up past her hips, skirts pasted by water reeds to her thighs, swimming then, to grapple with him, to pull up the son of her friend from such a grave. His face looks up endlessly. Echo now is to tumble with him, it is said. As if caught in a waterfall of timeless utterance.

It is the beginning, Polydoros says, from now on it will be this way. We will place the statues of the missing, all of them, along the hallowed ground of the thoroughfare. As we travel we will remember. Where are we going? Who has come this way? Polydoros and his newly chosen bride are forbidden to attend the rites of the dead during their nuptial year. They will put it out of their heads, this tragedy, lying down together to conceive a brilliant lively little son they will call sweet Labdakos, lucky father of the one to be named Laios, father to be of the one they will call Swollen Foot, Wise One, Oedipos. We pray for their good fortune.

Of all the generations Teiresias has seen, this disturbs him most. These were his childhood friends! Of all the generations, these are the lost who must wander homeless without a place to lay their dispirited heads.

Ameinius now lay coiled in an open jar wearing the thin clay boots Emporous the potter made for him. And at the heel of each were wings, papyrus-thin. He wore a new white toga and in his left hand, lightly, he held the curled fingers of his severed right one. A suicide must carry his own hand into the Underworld this way so that he might have some chance of pity, some slight chance of admission. In the urn, under Ameinius's head, was placed a stone, and in his mouth a coin for the ferrier. His mother placed it there. And beside him: a beautiful honey cake for the journey.

An old man is speaking now, while the funeral procession has come to a halt by the stones Polydoros has erected. Here gapes the mouth of the cave where others were once buried, long before our time, in antiquity. In Ameinius's home the workmen follow his parents' wishes; they make a modern resting place for him. The workmen move aside the chairs and couches; now they dig into the thick wall. While they labor, the funeral procession will make its way three times around the town, with the urn still open. We can see his features now as every day we saw them. Beside him a little food, and there his favorite childhood chariot and doll. The old man's voice is strong though we are not surprised to hear it quavering:

"How can we forget the first wail of this infant, his pinched pale face, the lavender opalescence of the broad slick cord that connected him to his mother, our exuberant passion at the sight of his small blue eyes staring out at us—as if we were indeed something to be honored.

"After his first cry, still bloody and covered with his birth wax, he was laid upon the ground in front of the house his grandfather built. The priest cast the scented petals about him in a snow-white flurry. His father chanted to him: Be close in your first moments, Ameinius, to the ground that holds the ones we loved. Be close to your mother's father, and your sister, our Medea, who has gone before you. Be close to my sister, your grandmothers, your great uncle Aries who walked with a limp and never said an unkind word but who had wisdom . . . we walk but a little while, Ameinius. Cherish these feet, these hands, and eyes, and sound of life that we have given you.

"We remember them, the new mother of Ameinius, the new father, this young overjoyed pair of lovers as they placed their forefingers into his palms. His tiny fingers curled so tightly around that together they laughed at the disproportion. We recall it well: how the new mother of Ameinius threw back her hair against her shoulders and her eyes flashed up. At husband, at son. Ameinius was bathed in the prized azure basin, drawn up and wrinkled like all new infants; like a little red frog he basked in fragrant waters and oils. We remember he did not cease his lusty cry until his windblown legs were drawn up and his arms drawn in and he was wrapped tightly as if in his mother again. And on his head, still molded from his journey, was placed his pointed red fabric cap.

"Look at him! she cried.

"The little jester, he laughed.

"Look at him! Look at him! she cried. He's here now. He's real! He's real!

"And his mother took him into their bed to nurse him. There she held his unsteady limbs.

"At the seventh-day celebration, after the ceremonial baths had been completed, as the family and servants stood in their finest clothes about the hearth, the young father stripped himself and with the infant in his arms ran shouting praise to Hera herself, Goddess of motherhood, Goddess of childbirth. Round and round the fire he ran, singing to his baby the song we know so well:

"Run swiftly and lightly with joy! he sang. Run with eagerness and anticipation. Run without fear, small light. Know you are loved. Know it in the soles of your feet, in the bouncing of your genitals with each step that you will take. Know our love in the roots of your hair as it swings on the wind. Never question it no matter the strife. Be wise and remember. Run swiftly and lightly, yearning for life as long as you live.

"We stand here and remember, we see these moments painted here on the death urn. It is so early to remember these things and make sums. We sing the same song for Ameinius, now in the Underworld to which he is borne. We pray for his admittance. We weep with these lovers who loved him."

The father is atremble. He relives it yet again. He will never tell his wife of the moment. She will never speak of her imagination of it while she waited for him to come back home. It haunts their separate lives now.

This father must perform the ritual. Indeed he must learn to hate the hand that killed his son. Can it be the little grubby hand of childhood suddenly grown, suddenly so suddenly disowned? The body has been laid out, washed, the women have filled the wounds with clay. Do not let this happen! No one can mistake the wounds for skin, yet how like-colored they are. Ameinius's face is pale yet radiant. How can that be? The arm lies extended over the brief table. His boy's hand upon the wooden cask, waiting. See how the fingers curl. Oh suicide. It is the only act for which one can never ask forgiveness for oneself.

His baby swaddled, he thinks on that. No, not that. He would take himself elsewhere, backward, backward into the beginnings of their small family, when life was an event of lusciousness, when all was hope and solidity. When to be away from his small son too long was to grieve for him. What is this wilderness of air through which his arms must swing? This is even worse than the worst he had imagined, braced himself for. A son lost in battle perhaps, he had feared that, feared his son's body might die before his, go inexplicably unclaimed, a feast for yellow wolves and birds. Can it be he has swung the ax into the air? It is the custom, it is required. How can his own son have done this to him? Perhaps if these sinners—five fingers, a palm, the tiny rivulets in each knuckle where time has passed through—perhaps if they are all rent from the one they have killed, perhaps the victim can go about his business with his dead friends, perhaps gain some relief at least, some happiness, some rest accompanied by his tiny spirit and theirs in the dampness of the Underworld. The wrist waits. The ax falls. A father wails.

Evening and the flute players accompany the mourners of the boy. The soft pelts of creatures, their dazed eyes, are gathered at the pond near the house. Their heads are swaying. There is nothing more desired, more feared than to love Narcissus. Unless it is to be Narcissus. Infatuation, you greatest trickster, you. The women relatives follow the body into the house lest the soul of Ameinius, small as the blossom of a violet, shaped like a man, winged at the shoulder and wild with new free form, might fly away, might take its lodgings in someone else, someone not of the family, someone alien and yet unborn. A bee with potent sting, a soul not settled. The sound of the urn snapping shut echoes through the house. The women are crying, as if they were birds in alarm. They would claim him still, gangly unfortunate one, almost a man, who yesterday ate at the table, sang quietly his anticipations, told an off-color joke and apologized most humbly, even sincerely. Together they laughed. Yes, to hear that joke right now, to hear it again and again.

and the meat the wine afterward,
almost a lingering of festivities

scratches in the cheeks: channels down which tears may run

hair torn like chaff

dawn breaks over Kithairon, and the little winged spirit
lifts up, falters a moment, hesitates. And then Ameinius,
is away.

It is well known that Mykenaean men and women from this period once stood on average at five feet ten inches tall—gigantic for the time. The tallest Mykenaean skeleton yet found measures five feet eleven and two-thirds. Men and women from nearby Thebes, however, reached merely an average of five feet six.

Looking out through cupped hands into the stars, Teiresias

watches the small streak of light like a fuse burning across the sky.

This then is real. Teiresias can see it. Again and again he has had this one dream, but he cannot understand it. The road unwinds beneath the little car, the billboards flying by like playing cards, the countryside springing up green and yellow, sprinkled with cattle black and white as wooden puzzles. The little boats rock at their moorings along the coastline; gray weathered houses shimmy like cardboard along the dunes and valleys. Twelve small panes are cut into the top of each window frame over yet another set of such glimmerings. Teiresias has had this dream so many times that he has counted them.

On the road, the back of a truck looms up before them. Each time it has been this way: the flatbed truck, the tarp poorly secured, lifting up. Oh human error! to have allowed them that one glimpse! Up it flew! Black triangle of canvas into blue air, and there: first the gigantic metal circle at the end, and then the four slate-gray radiating pinwheel metal fins. The women are laughing still, pulling alongside it now, barely noticing. But what is this long gray object, this cone? The flame-red car shoots past and passes once again over the center line. They look back shuddering; and they can see it, now and in their dreams, through the window of the truck's cab itself. Behind them, they can see the tip of the warhead barreling down the road, as if upon them. And off to one side, a white building with windows filled as if with frescoes. His light is brilliantly shining.

IV

The Pure Tone

Out of the pits and whorls of consciousness comes the sadness of fate. Silence, secret offender, has gobbled them up, kidney and bone. They are no more than pendants now: light upon a broken window shard. A brooch. The sculpted replica of a young man's head on an olive branch. Familiar stories now. Thousands of miles away, over oceanic distances of land and time, one blue *hippopotamos* sits beside a printed card and in the next cabinet a woman rides on the back of a bull—on a blue glass plaque.

Teiresias was a madman after his death, so the others said, speaking on and on of what he called memories when the others had none at all and saying they had all been a part of it. His first memory he would recount after his death, looking up at his companions who could not remember a thing, as he on his knees sniffed both blossoms and root of the asphodel, was that of watching his mother painting her breasts.

He remembered many things vividly from his youth: the prickly hedgehog caps the warriors wore, the hexameters of the sacred songs, the bison so prevalent when he was a boy, gone even before the year when he abruptly lost his sight. A plague of field mice came funneling back; this, too, they had had to endure. All right, all right, they said, if you must, then tell us again. It makes little difference now—to us, that is. Yes, yes, Teiresias, you foresaw the greatness of Heracles, the terrible Dionysian feast, the earthquake before the fall of Thebes, the victory of the Epigoni, the evacuation of Thebes. The rest are terrible bad dreams and you, Teiresias, were the unfortunate messenger. Yes, the generation that destroyed Thebes fought at Troy afterward. You know that, Teiresias, as you sit with this living man Odysseus, who has begun to shrivel with fear in the land of the dead. He would like to go home and finish the destruction of everything about which you even remotely knew and cared. Even the trade routes will be disrupted then. To think that trade routes could seem so personal. How bizarre. You are rent in two by your momentary and futile power. The longer you keep him here, the less effect he has on the world. Odysseus himself has helped call these people from your past, with the help of Circe's potion. You would watch the parade of sight and speech go on for an eternity. That is selfishness. And yes, you would keep them from his deeds. That is wisdom but with little consequence. Face the facts. You may know what will happen but there is little or nothing you can do. Is there no good to be derived from it? Is there nothing at all good about this man's visit to you? Ah, put aside your difficult thoughts for a time. Take a break from the dismal reality that is yours. Look at him.

Odysseus is aghast. Before him now is the beautiful Antigone, who was shut up in a cave for burying her own dead brother so that he, too, might go to the Underworld and not be torn apart in front of her by wolves.

"Did you see it as it would be?" Odysseus asks Teiresias. "Did you know what would happen to her?"

Teiresias sadly nods. *When the guard rolled the stone across, white gravel filled her throat, for all her crying in the dark. Her eyes slammed shut like two garage doors. She hanged herself with her scarf.* And now her brother says to her in the moment Odysseus has given them: "Why, why did you do it? I'd rather have been left unburied— though no other shade wishes this—than for you to have seen me already picked apart."

"Ah," Odysseus says, "a proud fine man."

"No, Odysseus," Teiresias says. "He loved his honor less than he loved her. He berates her for her blind bravery. Life has always been a complicated thing.

"In ancient Thebes, once a modern town not unlike your own, Odysseus, the clappers at the sides of doors were shaped like boots. This was to remind us of where we were going and its relationship to where we had been." A large yellow cat walks with its stumpy tail awag. *Here, kitty kitty. River Willow! Where have you been?*

Odysseus looks with admiration at the seer, but comprehension is not yet in the warrior's face.

"Shortly after 1350 B.C. Lake Kopais was drained by an extensive system of viaducts."

"Yes, we know that," Odysseus says. "We know of that."

"Leiriope was responsible," Teiresias says.

"Leiriope?"

"Narcissus's mother. Drained it after Narcissus drowned."

"Narcissus had a mother?"

Teiresias looks harshly at him now. "Doesn't everyone? Even this one coming here did."

"Who is it?" Odysseus asks.

"Need you ask?"

"Teiresias! Old friend," Oedipos says. "To think I once coveted your gold-knobbed blindman's cane, the one that bore my own face."

Teiresias is at the river, surrounded by shades. Here he draws a map in the dirt with a stick. This is the way it was, he says. Try to remember something for once. An immense, striped cat is licking at his feet. Well, he says, finally, to the beast: You remember it at least.

Only in death has his profession become a glorified thing. Teiresias can remember clearly the day Pentheus had his men tear down Teiresias's place of augury.

The world is made up more of common things anyway, Teiresias thinks. These are what we live: The stroll past the shop of the Egyptian butcher who had found special herbs for preserving meat even in the intense heat. The potter turning the wheel under hand and foot. The manicurist's special jokes, the way he laughed. For years here Teiresias has searched for his father—in vain. Eueres's transformation left little for the Underworld. The Underworld has no place for time. One by one Teiresias brings them out: the fragments of his world. "Are you still there?" he calls. "Are you still there?"

"Yes, yes," Odysseus cries. "I am waiting here!"

"Don't do it," Odysseus's own mother says. "Don't turn him loose from here. Listen to yourself for once, Teiresias. Stop following after Fate."

"I have to get home," Odysseus cries.

"You already are home," his mother says. "This is the best home you'll ever find."

"Are you still there?" Teiresias calls.

"I have to get home," Odysseus cries again. "Please don't anger me. Just point it out to me. I have responsibilities."

"Not you!" Teiresias growls. "Not you, Odysseus!"

"But I'm waiting!"

"Are you still there?" Teiresias calls repeatedly. "Yes, there you are."

At a point three thousand and forty years hence, in a land you have only dreamed, a barge makes its way across open sea, bearing a piece of the Acropolis. Perhaps most remarkable is the fact that in your whole life, Teiresias, you have only seen the Acropolis in dreams.

"So what?" Teiresias says. "Dreams are insignificant to you. To me they are intricate and living things."

"Pay attention," Zeus said to Teiresias. "And—eventually—one of us will try to raise you from the dead."

Zeus the Oak rolled his hands over you. He never beat you. He softened everything with the silkiness of living things. First he entered you by way of your eyes—all the golden liquid flowing out from his irises. His glance quickened the inner lining at the back of your skull and ran down into the swallowing of your throat, opening even the smallest channels of your interior. Then he entered you with the wafting musky scent of growing things. With his cultivation of the one pure tone he entered into your ears. And then he offered you the small brown meaty things that he had grown. He entered your thoughts by way of conversation and with stern chastisement for your way of having human words and human sentiments. And then, too, he entered you, relentlessly, with his cajoling and teasing and the barbed remark. By way of roots he tied you to the ground, you, a viscous, intelligent, and all-knowing thing. Finally he entered you by way of faithfulness and intent—deeply stated—without and within. "You are a very naughty girl," he laughed, "to let me enter you."

"Spank me," she said. "Spank me again."

And now: What was he? His pate, his shrunken breasts, his parts shriveled into something unrecognizable—these breasts, were they too small? or were they too large? male or female? Still, in memory, Emporous held him on his lap. Still, young love even after centuries went beyond these things. It was the one thing he had known with certainty about the present world, not past or future but the living reality of the here and now. Love was the one pure tone. It was the electricity that poured through the storm. It was like lightning pouring through a musical instrument. It was the perfect tone gone multiple and into song. It was something inconceivable. It was Zeus inside a note, then a series of them all at once in its waves, chord and discord, Zeus igniting emotion and activity at appointed hours, at random, whenever and however he chose. It was the fringe around the face of God gone benevolent as sometimes only Zeus could do. Yes, Teiresias said to himself, whatever had happened to him when he had been a woman had happened to other women, too. But, for the pure musical tone of a God, there had to be more than pleasure, Teiresias thought. There had to be the resurrection of humanity for the common driven immortal good. There had to be compassion, unending and significant.

So he remembered it throughout his life and there again in the Underworld, where after two hundred years of living blindness he could once again see. He remembered vividly what it was to die, the sensation of his tongue swelling in his throat and then going dead as a wooden cork to stop up not only his gagging but also the roar of life from body to head. Teiresias had explained it to his visitor.

Oddly, only Odysseus could see clearly here in the Underworld; and he, the great warrior, once brave and resplendent, was hysterical to get out of it. Odysseus would get it out of him, out of Teiresias the One Who Knew: the way out, away from the cloying dead, the looming experience that everyone around him here had most intimately known. Odysseus would have that answer anyway. And Hera, looking on, had been too preoccupied with her quarrel to understand the crux of what had gone on before. Teiresias had been spared—by the silence of Zeus, who through the darkness Teiresias could see, almost eternally, smiling warmly at him as he used to be, on that one day, when she, Teiresias, had had the nine parts of electrical pleasure most lavishly explained to her.

"You are a naughty girl," Zeus said.

"No," she said. "Don't blame me."

For this, Teiresias, you will never see your mother again, nor your father, nor your truest friends again. Not even in the Underworld. You will live an eternity and you will never once forget their passing. You will relive it again and again. Not even the River Styx will be able to rescue you.

Now say it.

Say what?

Say it.

What?

Say, thank you, Hera.

Thank you, Hera. Thank you very much.

First there came a sprouting of leaves.

Evolve! he cried, EVOLVE! EVOLVE! EVOLVE!

"So, this is evolution," she said.

The little boy's hand is slightly damp, plump only near the palm. The boy is only seven; and it is an instantaneous warmth—this small doughy hand in the blind man's own cold one. The little Mopsos likes to call him Grandfather, or Papa when he is moved or afraid; it matters little whether the old man is his grandfather or not. As it is, he has been like both a grandfather and a grandmother to him. The old man, this Teiresias, is listening for birds.

"What is it, Grandfather?" the little boy says. "Why do you stop like this on the road?"

"Because I can't see," Teiresias says.

"You never do, Grandfather."

"Yes, that's true," the old seer says. "I was just listening to find out what to expect—if you see what I mean."

"Did you hear anything?"

"No."

"You might have got us run over by a cart," Mopsos says.

"Shush now, little one."

"Papi, don't stop in the middle of the road!"

"Oh, all right, all right—you tell me when it's safe for an old man to cock his ear for one moment or two. It's up to you. You know I missed the sound of that bird just now—" There is a tugging at his arm and a dragging on it all the same. "Are you kicking at stones again?"

"Sorry, Grandfather."

"What kind of bird was it?"

"I didn't quite see."

"You were kicking at stones."

"Yes, Grandfather. I'm sorry."

"Try to recall it for me."

"It was an eagle."

"So you did see."

"Yes, I saw that it was an eagle flying straight up."

"Describe the shadow to me."

"I can't," Mopsos said. "The king's cart rushed behind us just when I saw it. I was trying to get you out of the way. The shadow went over the king's head, and his horses'. Then the bird cried and flew away. Could you hear it? Some of the other boys say they have a big nest now, on the mountainside. It was crying."

"No, no. I see it when you mention it."

"It was small and old."

"Ah," Teiresias said. "Are you absolutely sure?"

"What is it, Grandfather? Yes, it was old, just as you said."

"It means your ancient Grandfather is about to starve to death—and with the sun directly overhead."

"Papa!"

"It's lunchtime, Mopsos. Take me home. Don't let me be squished by a king."

"Does it mean that only? I can tell when you're worrying."

"Well, that's one thing," Teiresias said, squeezing the small reassuring hand where it wrapped around his other arm. "Remind me now," he said. "Remind me of these things later, after we eat. And one more thing— Which one is your mother? Manto or Historis? Which one is she?"

"Well, of course you know!" the little boy said indignantly.

"Just testing," the old man laughed. "You must always remember your mother." He laughed again, rejoicing silently in having been remembered both as mother and as father by the same two women who lived with him. It seemed a great joke on reality, the way things had been.

"Manto is my mama. She can see the future."

"I know, I know," he said. "And you begin to see it, too. I know it very well. I am a very lucky man to have your mama and you here to live with me. After lunch we'll have some serious bird-watching."

"I won't miss anything," the one called Mopsos said. "I never miss anything for you."

"No, that's true," the old one said. "No, you never do—"

"As far as you know," the boy laughed impishly.

"Yes that's right. As far as I know, you haven't made up the birds entirely. And the observatory."

"I would never do that."

"No. I never thought you would," Teiresias said. "I never ever did think it of you."

They were coming to the cottage now, he could feel the gravel quickening beneath his feet, and the small solid blocks of the animals' buildings jutting into the air currents eddying around them, then a mild rush of dark wind when they came to a street. The pleasant odor of his daughters' cookings encompassed him. They passed then under the stone that had so many times delivered his forehead a good knock. The sheepskin rug cushioned his feet, and then the woven one his daughters had made—his grandson Mopsos said it was red with a small black stripe. He had a fondness for the memory of red, and a distinct aversion. He was thinking of the first time he had experienced menstrual blood coming out between his legs after Hera had changed him from a man. It had been thick and red, almost black in places, and seeing it, it had seemed to be almost everywhere, actually running down his legs. At times he considered these things—when he considered his feet and where they had carried him already, onto the rug in particular. Now he put out his hand and the arm moved into it. Then he was down in the comfortable chair, the spoon in one hand, the good thick bowl in the other and the steam plunging into both nostrils, steady as hot sticks. "You wouldn't think it would get so cold at midday. It didn't used to get this cold," he said.

"Watch your bowl there, Father," Manto, his younger daughter, said. "It's quite full; you're tipping a little to the right."

"What happened today, Father?" Historis asked matter-of-factly. "Was it what you'd expect?"

Then a sudden maddening jerk at his leg made him jump, nearly sent the bowl out of his hand. "Hey there!"

"Oh, I'm sorry, Father," his older daughter cried.

"Historis! Your baby has pulled the hair right out of my leg."

"I'm lucky you didn't trample him," she said.

"Trample," he muttered. "Trample. You'd think I was a herd."

The little boy sleeps on a cot beside Teiresias's bed. And there, too, the little boy caresses the old man's hand, again and again, pressing his fingertips curiously along the ancient veins. There, on the back of his grandfather's hand, he learns by touch his grandfather's dreams. On the back of his grandfather's hand, in cords and veins, is an exact map of the streets of Thebes. After fifty years or so, the boy, a man, will discover it again in his memory. The image of his grandfather's hand will lead him in a mere few hours through a dark, moonless, and disheveled town, blown apart by earthquake and made a shambles by the attending ravages of war.

"Here is the first gate," the small Mopsos often says to his grandfather, "at the end of this string here in your hand. And here is the second gate here. And the seventh is the big one coming from your heart."

"Those aren't strings, little one," Teiresias says. "Not all of them. That one makes my finger work."

"It is a string," the little boy says. "And it's the fourth gate. It doesn't matter what makes your fingers work."

The hand hangs over the side of the bed, the boy studies it even in his sleep. In the middle of the night, at just the point when the old man must turn, as if predestined, to face the other way, the little one will awaken and crawl up into the bed with him. Innocently, he will wrap himself around the old Teiresias, resting the edge of his knee just so on the old man's hip, his face and chest pressed between the old man's shoulder blades, a large stuffed cat that his grandfather has given him tucked between his tummy and the old man's back. The little boy claims that the old man snores like fifty lions from Kithairon; the old man claims the little boy snores exactly like a mouse.

The boy has taught the old man many things, some by reminder, some by pure observation and reportage, some by encouragement. Perhaps the old man, too, is teaching the boy; that would be the usual way. But the man—ancient, blind, gifted in certain ways, and reliant on his two daughters and their children—has this one place in the hills for his auguries. After a rest, the old man and the boy go up to the mound of stones where sometimes the neighbors throw their rubble on the hill. They feel the wind rush about their faces. From time to time the old man feels his own hair stand straight up on the top of his head. He doesn't know why it gives him so much pleasure to put out his hand and feel the little boy's hair standing up in the wind, too. The cold heat of the sun beats red then blue, suffusing the lids of the old man's eyes; Hera has left him this. The old man has perched himself on his usual stone, his head in his hands now. And the little boy is pounding him on the back. "What is it? Grandfather. Tell me what it is."

The old man waves him away but cannot speak. Finally he tells the little boy what he saw when he heard of the eagle flying over the carriage earlier that day. The little boy sits beside him, stunned, rubbing gently the old man's veins unconsciously. "Do something, Papa. Can't we do something? For my friends."

"Well," he says. "I can't. I can't do anything. I've been awake all night; I can't do anything. It all started a long time ago." The little boy has touched his hand. It is just like a warm benevolent animal there, perched on the back of his hand. "You see, twenty-five years ago, our King Oedipos's father went to the oracle at Delphi after the birth of his first child, and the oracle gave him bad advice. Or rather, she gave him no advice. Not that King Laios would have listened to good advice. But on the word of the Delphic oracle, he took his own newborn little baby out of his wife's arms and sent it away to be killed—because of what the oracle had said."

"But what did the oracle say to the old king, Papi? Did you know him?"

"Yes, yes, I knew him. Until then I had been the seer for generations to the kings of Thebes. It was only that one time anyone went anywhere else. Who knows why he did it? Well, anyway, the oracle said the baby would grow up to kill him and marry his wife, the queen. The king decided to stop the situation before it got started, if you see what I mean."

"Papi!" The old man could feel the little boy's hands tightening on his arm.

"Oh, I shouldn't tell you these things," Teiresias said forlornly. "But you will know anyway, in your own eyes, I think. He tried to kill it. He was a madman, the old king. He had the baby's feet stabbed with a sword. He watched this himself, and then a servant was supposed to kill the baby while the king sat on his horse looking the other way. I will never understand where these people get off, expecting servants to do the foulest deeds—"

"Papa," the little boy said. "Don't start going on about servants and kings again."

"Yes, you're right," Teiresias said. "The old king was a young man then, with a beautiful new baby and a wife. He went to the worst oracle in all of Greece, and she told him a ridiculous story to amuse herself, maybe even in her malicious way to amuse me. Thereafter it all came true, one wretched deed after another. The baby was left to die. Can you imagine it? Asking a man to run daggers through a newborn baby's little feet, and then to chop off its head."

"Did he do it!?" Mopsos cried. "Did the servant chop off the baby's head?"

"No, no," Teiresias said. "The servant couldn't do it. He would never have cut the child's feet if the king hadn't been standing right there behind him and threatening him. Still, it was the most gruesome deed of his life; I don't expect the servant ever recovered from it."

"He shouldn't have done it anyway."

"Yes, yes, its true. No one should ever have done such a thing. But that's what some men are, brutes for life, all out for their own lives. Can you imagine anyone asking me to do such a thing? Of course not, it's obvious that I would rather die myself than cut up a newborn child—king's wishes, king's riches, or no. And so they do not ask. Your outside reflects your inside, Mopsos, and everyone will take what they can."

"Papa, I can't understand what you say. What happened to the baby? Stick to the point."

"Well, you've seen King Oedipos with his very slight limp. I knew it even before I went blind. Our own very sweet and kind, beloved king. That is your baby grown up—"

"The king?"

"Yes, raised by shepherds who found him, the poor little thing, bleeding to death as the sun was going down on the mountainside. Well, when he grew up, he decided to go off and seek his life. He said good-bye to the people who had raised him and in one short day trip came upon the old king's coach and his three men, and was again attacked by the old king's men—for sport, this time. It was a sort of hunting party, and the old king decided on the spur of the moment to join in. And so Oedipos killed the old king in self-defense, as any man would.

"Some people will tell you as time goes on that he was trying to rob old King Laios at the crossroads, but it's not so. He was not a robber, not Oedipos, not then, not now. He is the kind of man one takes things from, he is an innocent, raised by shepherds, with a king's blood. His father's father had something to do with shepherds, too; it's too bad Laios couldn't keep that gentler part of his heritage in mind. Anyway, Oedipos, by the hand of his own father, fell into a whole new way of life; and then Oedipos, without knowing it, had by his own hand now murdered his father who had twice tried to kill him—once knowledgeably, the other out of a general peevishness. There has been this condescending attitude, Mopsos, from rich to poor for a long time, but anyone can end up in any of it, rich or poor from moment to moment. It is always wise to have compassion and openness in your heart. Mopsos, I feel that you are not listening."

"You were speaking of compassion again, Grandfather. You have spoken of compassion many times. I get a little sleepy when you start it up again. It was the king I was interested in."

"Yes, yes," Teiresias said. "I suppose you were. Oedipos was a smart man, and simple, kind—unlike most people he would soon come to know. Weeks passed; of course, he thought nothing of having killed a stranger who had tried to hunt him down, screaming, 'Kill the stranger, kill the stranger,' with three other men, for no reason, like a wild boar. Then he came into Thebes one day by the high road and saw a monster there. The monster asked him the question it asked everyone. Answer or die. That was the way with this beast."

"Was it a hard riddle, Papi?"

"No, no," Teiresias said. "Not for the likes of you, riddle king. But for everyone else it was very, very difficult. Half the village was eaten by this monster because they were too scared to think. Well, Oedipos heard the question—what goes on four legs in the morning, two legs in the afternoon, and three in the evening?—and answered straight away. 'Why, that's easy, beast,' he said. 'It's a man.' At which point the monster choked on her own bad joke and died. The countryside was free. Oedipos rode into town on the backs of the people, a hero having answered the riddle of a monster. Soon he had been taken in by the queen, who had been made a widow not that much earlier—say several weeks, at the hands of Oedipos himself, unbeknownst to Oedipos, in self-defense.

"Now if you think back and consider the reaction a very young mother—she was just thirteen—might have had at having her first baby stolen away from her breast and, as she believed, murdered by her own husband, as he himself said to her, on the advice of a stinking, naked oracle and one of ill-repute—everyone else had relied upon me after I came of age. You can understand how it must have been for Jocasta all those years after that, submitting to the needs of this man. For twenty-five years she could not bear the sight of her husband for having done this thing to her and to her innocent little babe. By this time, she was not all that sorry to have suddenly lost the king, her husband, and his entire hunting party to marauders at the crossroads, as it was believed. She was certainly happy to see the people present such a fine, handsome, and gentle man as this Oedipos, their candidate for her new king. When she saw him it was as if she had been meant to love him all her life. They looked into each other's eyes and knew each other as if from the start. And that is how it was that Queen Jocasta inadvertently married her own son, and they had three children and were very, very happy indeed. The countryside prospered, and the people were content."

"Until now? Grandfather? Until now?"

"Until now. It's unfortunate, very unfortunate now, a kind of false understanding. A king may ask his people to do anything for him, even murder innocents and throw themselves into burning flames—"

"Burning fires? Did the servant have to do that, too?"

"That's another story. And, in return, his people may ask him to fix absolutely anything, so long as it's big, worthy of royal attention, beyond normal human means of fixing, so to speak— weather, pestilence, plagues. It's an entirely ridiculous set of expectations. It's the old dictum: If something goes wrong, Gods play and man must pay. Do you see what I mean?"

"Maybe. Well, I think so, Papa. Maybe not."

"Well, little one," Teiresias said. "As you know, the rain has stopped for months; and it is cold, then hot, then cold. The weather is erratic and the crops grow dead, people begin to be worried and thin. Their little children are hungry, some are sick. Everyone has gone to the king. He is frantic with worry, that something in the village has caused this thing. He has sworn to eradicate it."

"Papi, Papi— Eradicate? What does it mean?"

"Remove, but quick, and thoroughly. To the root. Get rid of it. That's what it means. There were several points where it could have been stopped—all this murdering."

"Like at the beginning, the king should never have married the first queen?"

"Well now," Teiresias said, looking into the vast regions of mind and reality, hearing the little boy's clear, high, and innocent voice like the sound of a flute piercing sweetly and distinctly the clear, cold, vaporous air. "I never thought of that. I never thought of it, it's so true. That would have stopped the whole thing, come to think of it. It's true it wasn't a good match. The king could never be responsible to her. He was so insignificant. He had no substance to him, nothing deeply interesting, but she wasn't a bad woman, she only wanted to be loved and attended to. It was a bad match, and she could never stop trying to control his every move, trying to make him attend to her the way she thought a loving husband might. But she was more and more cruel and unthinking, saying terrible things, denying the pleasantness of every moment, denying any attempt he made to change. Anyway, they fought from the first, tooth and tong. It was an arranged marriage. I'm against arranged marriages. You should be, too. But all the same, they did marry, and the baby was born. So what could have been done?

"Already there are murmurings that she will be replaced at Delphi. Apollo may replace her entirely, I don't know. I can see it now, Delphi, a place where anyone may turn for guidance, for succor; even slaves will be set free if they can make the journey there. This oracle will be replaced by other women under the direction of Apollo, wiser women, but not the likes of her. Anyway, Mopsos, she gave King Laios a riddle, not a koan, and then she told him what to do."

"He didn't have to listen to the oracle?"

"Well," the old man laughed, considering again. "It's very hard not to listen to an oracle, if I do say so myself. Generally, if it's a good oracle, it's better to listen than not. But you're right, he didn't have to listen. Yes, that's true, too. That's very good, they could have listened, like their forefathers, to me instead.

What an irresponsible use of knowledge, to send the baby's father off that way, with nothing but a puzzle like that. You're right, he shouldn't have listened and he shouldn't have gone. But, it could have happened to anyone. Even I was duped as a child by that Delphic frenzy. I thought I was worthless for half a century at least."

"But you didn't kill any babies because of it."

"Certainly not."

"Grandfather, he didn't have to take the baby away."

"That's right," Teiresias said. "It is a great sin to kill or maim your own child. It's enough of a sin to bring murder down on your own self, but your entire line, and your own infant—"

"He could have gone away."

"He could have gone away!" Teiresias shouted. "He could have gone away!"

"It's all right, Grandfather. It's all right."

"No, I never thought of that," Teiresias said. "King or not, Laios could have gone away! At least he would have had his own integrity. His relationship was not good with the wife anyway. He should have accepted it. The boy, if the oracle was right, was going to kill him anyway. He had two choices, to live as happily as possible with his wife and child—which was not possible even before the child was born; and the other was to go away. I never thought of that! If a thing is good, it will follow you. And if it's not, you have not brought yourself into the sin of piercing your own child's feet, of separating a mother from her baby, of taking an innocent life. He could have packed up the small things he cared for and gone away. Ah, but quickly, otherwise he might have come to love the child. Oh, to leave a child behind is the most difficult thing, if you have a soul. But still—"

"Grandfather?"

"Why, I ask myself, have I not done this same thing in my life? I had no one to hold me back. Why have I not taken the middle road, packed you up and gone away, at least for a time, and returned you to your mother when you needed her? Why didn't I go and allow those who needed me to follow me? All my life I've lived like a caged animal, sitting here because of my responsibilities lest anyone want to come and speak with me. Now I am an old man and only once have I been to see the sea. I was a little boy then, I went with my father just shortly before he was killed. Can you believe it? Now I am blind, and I will never see the sea. I live in Greece but I've never been to Greece. I've only been to Thebes. Thebes is not Greece. Thebes is only Thebes. I went to Delphi, it was beautiful—but already the onion lady spat at me. I was only a little child." He had begun to whine now, audibly; he was aware of it, but his heart was sore and he could not stop himself.

"Don't be sad now, Grandfather. You said yourself she was a hoax. Don't be sad. She probably knew how great you were. Please tell me, I don't understand what it means that the eagle's shadow overtook the cart."

The old man felt his head rolling in the cradle of his own two hands, a polished, hollow skull rolling back and forth in his palms in the complete dark. It was as if he could look at it there in his hands surrounded by the pinpoints of stars, impermanence and the finality penetrating everything he knew.

The little boy was sitting beside him now. He could feel the child's arm go around his waist, and the small head resting itself in the crook of his elbow, the warm breath at his side. "Papa? Is it very bad?"

"Yes, oh yes," the old man sighed, gathering himself. "The people are demanding that the evil spirit, whatever it is, be removed from Thebes. The oracle at Delphi swears it is the cause of the drought, this evil thing which should be found out. I say the drought is because of the Gods, not because of some silly circumstance of man. Zeus is preoccupied with something else—one of his love affairs. He's taken thunder and lightning, rain, elsewhere. And with human beings, Zeus refuses to use a guiding hand. Without a guide, the people turn on themselves. I'm sorry to tell you, my little one. Your two little playmates will be homeless soon, their father blind, their mama dead, my little one." The little boy's lip was trembling against his cheek, the arms around his neck. "This work is too hard for you," Teiresias said. "You are a little boy. You should grow up like other boys, live in the world where you don't have to know such terrible things. Here there is nothing to be done about it, it can only be foreseen."

"Papi, I would know anyway! Same as everyone else in a few weeks. Papi, stop crying now."

"Oedipos has called me to tell him what is going on. If he'd called me sooner, or his father had, perhaps none of this would have happened. I think that repugnant oracle at Delphi is playing games. She thinks it sport to bring down Thebes—because of me, I suspect. She can see no further than her sleeve."

"But the oracle at Delphi has no sleeves, she is always naked, Papi. That's what you said."

"That's exactly what I mean, my boy. That is exactly what I mean."

"Please Papa," Mopsos pleaded, "tell my friends' papa what to do. Tell him to go away quick and start again. Like Laios should have done. It isn't the same everywhere, is it, Papi?"

"No, no, little one. It's not the same everywhere, and yet many things are the same. Oedipos and Jocasta will think they carry their guilt with them, yet their guilt is the biggest crime of all for what it is about to do. It is better to accept themselves, even forgive themselves and start anew. It is possible to start over, if simply, in another place, or if you are strong enough, in the same place. There are sometimes different kinds of people in different locales. Think about it, little one, maybe we ourselves could go with them, someplace else. It is surprising who will follow you. But, little one, don't hope too hard. It is very difficult for a man who has been injured as an innocent child not to turn around and injure himself. From now on, Thebes will be tumbling down."

And so he had gone to tell them the story privately. "Listen to me," he said to Oedipos. "Try to put your trust in me. Listen for once. Don't just react to what I know. Sit back and listen for the way, Oedipos. It's not your fault. Forgive yourself. It's not your fault."

But Oedipos, crying and weeping, threw him out bodily at the hands of guards. Teiresias felt the boy approach him before he even knew where he had landed. He was hunched over himself, wheezing painfully with a burn inside that threatened to break him up. He had a bruise up and down one side, and his ribs—several had broken up against one of the columns at the entry to the palace. The little boy was crying. "Papa, why have they treated you like this when you've only tried to help them out?" Perhaps his brittle elbow would never completely heal, he thought. By the pain in it and the way the arm hung at such a funny angle in his sleeve, he felt this to be true.

From the palace steps, with the little boy comforting him, he could hear even now Jocasta shouting and crying in the far corner of their elegant habitat, not so far from where he lay, and Oedipos shouting back at her. It did not take much for Teiresias to see the next few days, as he sat there on the steps. He could see it as if with his own eyes: the mother of Mopsos's little friends hanging by a scarf as Oedipos pressed his face sobbing into her dead skirts. And there on the bed, the brooch he had given her at their wedding, the bright pin attracted in the moment of consequence to the centers of his eyes and the thrust of grief to drive it in, twice. Soon the little children would be their father's only friend. If only they had had some way to understand that even this ludicrous situation might have been a gift to everyone rather than a sin. The drought might have finished as droughts will, and the town gone on in splendor, spiraling upward rather than wrapped eternally on the grinding of the horizontal wheel.

Now they were descending, all of them, and the fault was not in what they'd done but how they'd seen it and themselves. Was there no guidance anywhere for any one of them? And Teiresias? No one would listen to him. He was a seer without a God, though he would have accepted one, willingly. If a God had backed him, then the people might have listened to him; he might have had a purpose in his life. In his time, no such God had appeared. No such God cared about him, or the likes of him, any of human kind. He cast himself, even as the boy helped him home, into the future for comforting.

A bitter memory comes back as frequently as a bad dream: Teiresias has aged at the hands of Gods, at the thought of his Thebes. Again he is reliving his childhood days. His hands are crepe, flowing. His sight is in the end of a stick that fingers its way among pebbles and the leavings of dogs. The sun is hot on the top of his head. Yet, what is that in the unrelenting darkness, that gnawing of stones? A foot on the path? Not his own. Then another. Mopsos has gone off into the brush for one moment. The sound of water, a streamlet, against boulders, crushes gravel and sand. Something is on the path approaching rapidly—most certainly information and fear. Perhaps a bad dream.

Much nearer, coming straight on, so it seems, swinging wide and encompassing every bit in its path. Fierce stammering. From the underbrush his young guide's ignorant sojournings, beatific whistlings from the distant pursed lips, the sound of water whizzing through air. Once, while a boy, Teiresias took such pleasure in making water in open air. Teiresias is lost now in the overriding sound of the bruising of gravel. He can think of nothing else. He is afraid.

Old, blind, withered, farting like a badly fed stove, with a roar of apprehension in the gut. This, his own accompaniment to his young guide's distant songs. *Where are that little boy's ears? Can he not hear the wise man's shouts for help?*

And then he has fallen, hit as if with a stone. "Can't you see I'm blind?"

"Can't you see I'm blind," he hears.

"Echo, Echo is that you?"

"Don't be a fool, man. It's me, Oedipos."

"Oedipos!"

"Teiresias? Is that you again?"

The prophet's own voice comes back to him. How time shimmies and sways. Once he imagined the occasion of his own death and understood not one portion of it, it was so far ahead of him, only a blur. Now it is so far behind that it looks nearly the same. Yes, he was old when he made the change. Old. He was more than ready five generations after his birth, and yet he lived two more. Ancient Teiresias. He was still a child when he foresaw the end of civilization as he knew it, the end of Thebes; now he claims a ponderous age: three thousand and eighty-five. When did it happen? Oh—at a hundred and fifty eight or so.

Make the lines distinct! Somewhere among the thirsty dead, he sees a pheasant strutting on a long green lawn.

Even Odysseus, a hardened man, noted the additional trembling in the already-shaken frame. "Old man," he said, sitting down beside him, forgetting for a time both himself and his fearful state, his responsibilities. "Old man," he said. "Don't take it so hard."

The quartz eyes turn up, frightening.

"What would you have me do? In all my life I have had only one true friend, and there he has gone into oblivion."

"There now."

"Finally I have understood it," he says.

"What is it?"

"Why death—I have understood the reason for it."

"What is it? Tell me now, if you can."

"The reason for it is apparent. For all my foolishness, I never saw it even in my sleep. Now here I am without the full effect. It is as if I had taken a dram of hot juice and left out the yeast. So what," he whined bitterly to himself. "So what."

Odysseus laid his living hand on the gauze of centuries and felt the upheaval of the wise man's back. "Worse has happened," he said.

"I have lived it all," Teiresias moaned. "I imagined them—as though they were my own—each moment of everyone's grief."

"It's over now," Odysseus said. "Let yourself rest."

"Oddly enough," Teiresias said, "looking back, you'd think I'd think it bountiful, that in some way I'd be pleased—"

"Lie down and rest," Odysseus said again, most gently.

The ancient shade lifted himself up most violently then. "Rest? Rest? What do you think we've been talking about?" Then Teiresias lurched at him so quickly that the great warrior threw up his arm as if to ward off an owl flying at his face.

The arms of Teiresias's robe flapped over the warrior's head. "Haven't you been listening? How can you be the leader of men when you can't remember a thing? All this interminable time since you came, I have been telling you again and again. That is my dilemma, that is my stone of Sisyphus, that is the crow that eats my liver out. Must I be more specific than that? It's no wonder you people wander about the earth making assaults on the innocent, leaving your loved ones to similar fates. You've no more memory of history than that river over there, or the lifeless ones who drink from it.

"You, you who have thrown little children off the battlements in the name of stopping war, you come to me who has remembered it, you ask me the way home. I tell you: Cure yourself of the thirst for blood, and you will find yourself at home in front of a fire with your slippers on. Cure yourself."

"Please stop," Odysseus quavered, crouched still in the stones. "I will, I will do as you say immediately. Thank you so much, Prince of Wisdom, Prince of Thebes."

Teiresias stared at him in disbelief. "You will do it, smooth talker? You, Odysseus? Animals have more tenderness. You will wander a thousand days and nights following the sun, and when you arrive home you will slaughter the boys and brothers of your own countrymen. Get out of my sight," he said. And then he wept, hysterically, "Such as it is."

"But how?! How? I don't know the way out."

Again I thought it, again across the mist she came and through it, as small and beautiful, as dark as in my dreams. I held out my arms. My

121

mother embraced me, and I brushed her hair with my hand at the back
of her head. I wept, even at my age. "Well?" she said. "Well," she
laughed, "is a hole with water in it. Your father played such games."

There were stirrings in the house that now came into his awareness. Teiresias again could hear the sound of women murmuring and the muffled notes of platters being quietly set together on a wooden table. Water moved through the drains and pipes. The tiny figure of his mother floated at the edges of the room. He saw her more clearly then as she leaned over the hearth and, having stirred the fire up so quietly, the light went up against her face. Frail, silent, lovely, she moved away then toward the staircase and halfway up she turned. He thought he noted relief in her face, affection, as she stood there gazing on against the light. He saw in her a tenderness that was not different from his own; he felt a union between them, though he could not know whether she had felt the exchange. She had dressed to come downstairs, and he could see in the orange firelight that she had built, and that now cast itself so fully upon her, her perfectly rounded serenity.

Every man, woman, and child wanted to rest his or her head there for comforting, secure in the knowledge that this God, the supreme God among many Gods, would not let anything evil touch you, so long as your head was on his chest. Everyone wanted it. Even while Teiresias spoke with Zeus, he had the sensation of being at rest. His old voice softened and became more melodic, as the God's golden eyes sent a kind of liquid warmth through even the seer's blind orbs. Of course, there was no hope of Zeus actually doing anything for anyone. Well and then, there was only hope; there was never any actuality, Teiresias reminded himself. Zeus had no concern with human beings, except playful ones. It was: Do as I say, not as I do.

"How can I be a better God?" Zeus asked most unexpectedly.

"You're not a God, to me."

"No, you're just upset. Tell me. Maybe I could change a little bit."

"I told you how I feel."

"Is it true?" Zeus said. "What can I do?"

"It's impossible. You would need love great enough to care for fleas."

"Right," Zeus laughed. "You are the most amusing man I know—not that I know many of them. Jump on my arm, Teiresias," he laughed. "We'll see how I care. And my life—what a travesty. What can I do? Hera won't even speak to me," he said yet once again. "What can I do? My life is wretched with her. More horrible than you know."

"We're not talking about your wife. You've got bigger responsibilities. Look at you. You're like a pendulum—swinging back and forth."

"A pendulum?"

"Pendulum. Later on it's hooked up with the passage of time."

"Oh. Something to do with your father, I suppose."

"A descendant of sorts," Teiresias said. "Maybe you like it, maybe you like it deep inside, having your life be such a travesty it takes over the whole of your experience. Maybe it's good. At least you know what to expect. She keeps you on your knees. Really, I'm serious, maybe it's a good thing. Otherwise, who knows what you might do."

"Don't be stupid," Zeus said. "Don't belittle my intelligence. What can I do?"

"I don't know," Teiresias said. "I think you should continue with her. Her ideas are changing."

"Stay?!"

"Until you have to leave. I don't know."

"I just don't know," Zeus mimicked him. "I brought you here for your knowledge. A little advice."

"All right," Teiresias said. "If you consider the impermanence of all things, you can see that it makes little difference whether you stay, or not, in a situation where you are belittled day and night and are cut for your deepest kindnesses. I mean that—you may as well stay as leave, if you're not going to change. I can't tell you what to do. It's all in how you look at it."

"Impermanence?" Zeus asked, serious for perhaps the first time.

"Everything dies eventually," Teiresias said. "Everything changes anyway. If you were human I would say there is hope in that. Perhaps it's good to stay with Hera—with that attitude. Or perhaps it's good to move on. I can't say what it means to you. It may be unprecedented, leaving Hera behind, but it is possible. Maybe it would be good for her, too. I'm not saying it would be easy. You will feel like your arm has been wrenched off. But other things will appear. After you leave her to her own development, many things will become possible. In the new world there will be one God with many arms. If it offendeth thee . . . "

"What did you say?"

"Oh, who knows? It's an unfortunate part of my trade."

"What were you saying?" Zeus asked again.

"I was saying—maybe you would find happiness in a new way of being. You might be able to do something for someone else, build a dynamic philosophy, raise all the world's children in a loving atmosphere, change the world. You have enough power, you could do almost anything. Invest the wealth of your knowledge in stopping misery, or at least in understanding or fighting it. Right now, you're not much better than Sisyphus. It's demeaning, living a life like that. Even if it looks good from the outside—which it doesn't, by the way; your wife tells all her friends everything; and she's nearly as powerful, and lost. All that matters is that you are able to change with her, or without her. That there is growth. Everything comes to an end eventually; yet, in that, it grows. There are many ways to protect what's yours. What do you want your existence to be?"

"What dies?" Zeus said indignantly. "Mere men possibly. Mere men die. Gods don't die."

Then the great God Zeus sat down again at Teiresias's suggestion and was told that whole civilizations would fade away, even everything they knew and were. That even their language would have to be resurrected by specialists. That most living people in future generations would not even know the names of the Gods that then were.

"Ah well," Zeus laughed hurriedly. "So long as *we* know who we are, that's the important thing."

Teiresias said nothing for a time, until Zeus through the darkness pressed him on. "All right," Zeus said. "I know for a fact you've seen something that I don't want to hear. Tell me about it now."

"I suppose," Teiresias said, "you're going to torture me for giving you what you request. I suppose it's inevitable."

"No, no," Zeus laughed. "That's all in my past. I'm trying to be a little more understanding now. Especially with you. You're the only one who's changed with me; I didn't have to do all the work."

"It isn't funny," Teiresias said, suddenly incensed, and torn between both sexes, present and past. "Talking about it like that isn't funny. Stop right now. Try to take me seriously for once."

"No, you're right, I'm sorry. It's not funny at all. I'm sorry," Zeus admitted rather curtly.

"But if you torture me, or anyone I care about, I'll never tell you another thing. You'll never torture my family."

"All right," Zeus said.

"It isn't something pleasant, I'm telling you now."

"I promise," Zeus said.

"Is it a serious promise? One you really mean? I've seen your work."

"It's a serious promise," the great God Zeus said. "I swear—if I promise you something, Teiresias—I swear it will be."

"All right," Teiresias said. "All right.

"I was sitting in my chair—I must have eaten something peculiar, often that will start me up—and then, before I knew it, I saw three new Gods— You weren't there—" Teiresias hesitated then.

"So we have three new Gods, do we? Where do they sit in the banquet house?"

"One is the God of impermanence, the other is the God of everlasting life, the third is the all-consuming God."

"And what did I look like in the dream? Which God was I?"

"As I've said, you weren't in the dream. Their names were Buddha, the Son of Man, and a man called Mohammed. There was an old God alongside of them, a Hebraic God. There may be others I haven't yet seen. I don't always see side to side. The new Gods were all in human form. Try to understand: You weren't in the dream. You weren't in the world anymore—except as a story, I'm afraid, that a few people told from time to time."

"In awe. They couldn't see me anymore."

"Not really."

"What do you mean I wasn't in the world anymore?"

"I'm sorry. You didn't exist. Not only were you dead, no one believed you'd ever lived. You were a story for amusement, or for information about the way another civilization lived and died, as you did. Try to think," Teiresias said. "Try to resurrect yourself."

"Died?"

"Died. In the future they will have thunder and lightning still, and all the other things you mean here; and they will not need you. I'm sorry to be so blunt. It was a dream of the future I had. I don't control what I dream."

Zeus leaned back, and Teiresias could hear his angry breath pouring out his nostrils in gale-force winds. Whole towns were swept into the center of him. "You promised," Teiresias said, "not to take it out on me. Or mine."

"Go on," Zeus said. And then Teiresias heard nothing. The world was becalmed.

"Shall I go on?"

"This is ridiculous," Zeus finally said. "Who cares what men think of me? You're talking about a transformation of ants." Teiresias heard a sigh. Waters were parted that had never been so before. "What were the names of these heretics?" Zeus said too quietly. "And where are their ecstatic cults?"

"You can't wipe them out," Teiresias said. "The three new ones don't exist yet; they won't exist for another thousand years, at least. Each one will be a human being, or a God in one, with—" and Teiresias swallowed hard, treading dangerous ground. If only he had been able to see the face of the being next to him. As it was he had merely to cast about in himself, listen to the shifting next to him. He went quietly on. "Each will be endowed with the powers of prophesy; something which—as you know—you have not yet done for yourself. Each Human-God shows human beings the way—with prophesy; each one of them is, or is linked to, a benevolent guiding force. They will replace you—as things look now to me. Along with the old God. He already exists."

"Oh," Zeus said. And stunned, he said it again, "Oh." His face was immovable then, for he had come in some way to believe in this seer. "Why should I care what men think of me? A mere man like yourself will represent Gods to mere men? As you yourself are doing now?"

Teiresias humbly said, "Not as I am doing. All my life I have only been a channel, perhaps I will always be. We are not talking about me here. Try to listen a little more carefully. In the dream, the one God, a young human prince, is nearly grown when he learns that human beings die. He is a little like you. He will say the same thing you have said when he is told of death. He will be so stunned, he will say only, 'Oh.' The sound of his own astonishment will echo in his mind for what will seem to him like a hundred grieving years. And then it will become a chant; it will stun him into a transformation. Millions will follow him—and numbers will not matter to him. The human beings who follow him will live one life after another, reborn after each death, again and again, improving or descending in significance in different forms, depending upon what they've done. They won't truly die. But you, you I'm afraid will be gone."

"This is ridiculous," Zeus said again. "It's the transformation of insects into Gods."

"I wouldn't know," Teiresias said. "I wouldn't know how you might think of us. Do you want me to go on?"

"Yes," came the now-familiar voice.

"All right," Teiresias said. "If you're sure?"

"Yes," came the voice again.

"I saw the other one, the son of everlasting life, the human son, have the same look in his eyes when his God let human men torture him and kill him. 'Oh,' he will say. 'Oh.' His father, not a human but a God—like you—will seem to sacrifice him, for the sake of human beings, not for himself. The men will nail his hands and feet to two logs and hang him there to die. This treatment is not, I might say, unlike what's happened to some of your friends when they've argued with you. Often you've taken a most human way. And then the human son of the God will come back to life again."

"I can't take it in," Zeus said. "He is brought back to life. Go slowly. He was a bad son?"

"No, perfect."

"I can't take it in." Zeus sat a long while silently. Teiresias could hear him breathing like a big bull about to sweep innocence to sea. "I have to do something," Zeus said. "I have to do something. I am entirely gone? The worst part is I know you've never been wrong. Still, you are human, you could make a mistake."

"You could change your relationship to human beings," Teiresias said. "I've been trying to think about it for you. That may be the only way. Already there has been one named Abraham."

"Ah, I have heard of him. The man whose God asked him to kill his own little son. In the end it was only a test."

"Only a test," Teiresias said. "Yet the test exists in the reality of the mind. Until his hand was stayed, the terror that lived in his little boy's eyes! It lives there still. These men would do anything for their God. You have heard of Job?"

"What kind of God would ask a man to do such a thing?"

"You would go further. You would exact the crime yourself."

"Not I."

"There is no man who is not a son, no woman not once a child. You yourself killed your father and your mother. It does not bode well for you."

"It is a succession," Zeus said. "Besides, your argument doesn't hold. Our parents were parentless. They were of the old order. We do what we have to do—to save the world. As you yourself said."

"Some will say the parents of your parents were born even of these other religions, or of others yet to be known. They will say that yours is an heretical cult. You have not one man who will stand in your defense."

"A God has no need of defense."

"That is true."

"Why do you say these contradictory things? Why do you say, 'No human sacrifice,' and throw the story of Abraham at me? When Abraham's God destroys one of his men, piece by piece, as slowly as even I might have done, to win a bet. What was his name?"

"Lot."

"And the other one you mention, one of the ones to come, allows his own son to be sacrificed."

"Not to win a bet. There is no need to chain human beings to the mountainside and call in an eternity of birds to peck their livers out. That is something humans do for themselves. Unfortunately, there are volunteers for all means of human annihilation and sacrifice."

"So you think I'm nothing then."

"I offer you an answer if you are listening."

"I said you think I am nothing then, in the future I mean."

"Merely circumstance, we watch now as it proceeds. I say only this, if you turn again to human sacrifice you are a fallen God. That's the way I see it. I do not address the others. They are born of a different time and place. I can't make you see that what they do is sprung from benevolence. It is not sprung from rage. Rage is a reaction bound to a point in time. Rage is not a timeless thing. It devours itself again and again, makes way for change. If you are to be timeless, you must put away rage. Rage is a human thing."

"I will never understand it; you, who have been so many ages and even sexes, give credence to human beings who have been next to nothing themselves."

"You forget, I am only that myself. I have never claimed to be otherwise. Gods do not follow after human beings, they are timeless, they go before. I myself prefer, even without sight, to follow after the animals in these times, to watch them soar."

"I will never ever understand it."

"You are back where we began. I give you credit for trying. Human followers may misinterpret what Gods have said and done, act falsely in their names. It is inevitable. Zeus, a river may carry a boat if it wishes to. In the future the makers of boats may change the boat or even the river in its course. The existence of the river, however changed, or even denied, will not go away. It will be transformed."

"We have already had that in Hercules."

"Perhaps then you understand the seriousness of your case. Perhaps you will find your answer in what I, a mere human, have said to you. For all my transmutations, I do not understand the intricacies of all worlds. If I can be transformed at your hand, you can be transformed at your own. You have already done it, but your purpose must be different. Do not step forward or backward. Flower from within."

"You ask me to do the impossible. You are talking to the wrong one."

"Maybe you are wrong. Maybe you will persevere." Teiresias turned then toward a renewed nervousness. "Now that we are speaking like this. Now that you sit beside me with, I sense, your head in your hands—"

"How can you see it?"

"I felt it to be so. I would like to ask you one selfish question, Zeus, selfish because all my life I've been wanting an answer for it."

"What is it you want?" Zeus said, with an irritation barely concealed in his voice.

"It's nothing I want. Well, this question haunts me—I've had this question for you for a long time."

"What is it, I said."

"Well, I've been wondering if you could help me understand something related to our discussion—why do you feel men must die? Could you answer that one thing for me? It might help me see the solution for all of us and for you a little more clearly now."

"How should I know, man," Zeus said angrily. "If I'm so insignificant, why don't you ask one of these new Gods? Or this God of Abraham, he's already hanging around."

Teiresias could hear Zeus drumming his hands on something hard. He realized then that Zeus had already dismissed him, although they sat together still in the same room. And then the immense booming voice:

"That's it!" Zeus cried, thinking aloud. "That's definitely it. That's what I need—a son. A human son who will lead the world in worshiping me."

"But you've missed my point," Teiresias yelped as he was hurriedly ushered out. "I've been trying to tell you how to help yourself." And then in the hall, "Good grief," he cried.

"I need a human son," Zeus was muttering behind him. The gateway to the Gods fell closed, a chilling current of air at his back just as Mopsos's tender little boy took his arm again, much as his grandson Mopsos himself had done not that many tens of years ago. The little boy's voice was not unlike his father's, though it carried its own unique sweet quality.

"What's the matter, Papi?"

"Oh no," Teiresias said, struck with his own stupidity. "Oh no."

"What is it, Papa?" Mopsos's boy said again.

"I forgot to tell him about the virgin birth," Teiresias said, more to himself than to this child who was so gently guiding him. "I forgot to tell him part of the dream. I forgot, and now it's too late to contact him."

"Don't worry, Papi," the child said to him. "You're not a failure. There's always tomorrow, isn't there?"

"Perhaps," Teiresias said, patting the little hand on his arm. "In some things. He wouldn't have understood it anyway. He doesn't understand about the continuance of things." Teiresias would have to wait until he was summoned again. And by then, knowing Zeus, Zeus would surely have started something up in trying to redeem himself.

All alone, and in a complete quandary, "Oh," Zeus said.

What it is to make love to Zeus—especially if you are newly born into life as a woman, yet again after such long passage, and your previous life is gone—is perhaps easy to experience, but not so easy to describe. Now she knew what it was that the others who had been with him had felt. It was as if she could make love to him eternally. He was the God of fertility and there was, she saw now, reason for it. It was not just the way of his body, nor its compelling nature; it was the way he used his hands, the way he brought his fingertips, forefinger and thumb, down each breast in a line that brought her painted nipples into his lips. It was the way he put himself between her breasts. It was the way he told her what to do, with and without saying it. It was the way he grimaced when he put himself in her mouth and held the back of her head. It was the way he entered her matter-of-factly and she wrapped her arms and legs around him, as if it was not sex they were having but love. It was how brief it was. It was not three hundred years. It seemed to her, oddly, the most human experience.

"You promised me you wouldn't disappear," she said.

"I won't," he said. "I won't."

"Do you promise it? No matter what happens with me or anyone else?"

"I do," Zeus said. "I promise you."

Zeus was seated when Teiresias came in, summoned to attend to whatever was worrying the God. This time Teiresias could see the God quite well: the thick black hair to the shoulders, the hair going a brilliant silver on his chest as well as on his head. The softness of it seemed to call out to all mankind. He was going slightly thick in the face, and in the chest. "Teiresias—" Zeus said. But as Zeus glanced up to greet his seer, the God's mouth dropped open. "What happened to you?'

"Your wife came across me at a bad moment. I was irritable, I drove apart two snakes."

"Again? And they were making love?"

"That's right."

"She does get irritated."

"I would have thought it more your disposition to defend the act of procreation, even more than Hera's," Teiresias said.

"Good heavens," Zeus said, staring at Teiresias's new form. "She certainly let you have your beauty. You know, I don't think I ever saw you when you were in this form before. You weren't half bad-looking as a man, of course; but, I must say, I prefer you now. And I see you've painted your breasts. There's something about the way human women wear their robes."

"Well," Teiresias said self-consciously. "She also let me have my sight again. Hera can be quite kind, you know. At times.

Maybe we shouldn't talk about it. I'm not quite adjusted to being this way. And the paint—I watched my mother doing it for a long time. Even as she aged, her breasts remained beautiful."

"As yours will," Zeus said flamboyantly. "Sit down, sit down. As everyone knows, age has little to do with beauty. Some women grow more attractive as they age, they ripen beautifully. I would rather have an older, beautifully confident woman in my arms," Zeus said, "than a silly young one."

"I didn't know that about you," Teiresias said rather curtly. "You had a reason for calling on me, I suppose."

She had covered her breasts with the northern rose—for its innocence, and perhaps for protection. Now she covered them with her arms. Her mother and many of the other women she had thought respectable had worn a similar pattern; although Teiresias thought, none of them had drawn roses, nor so delicately. She had painted the entire exposed part of her chest chalk-white, as if it were fabric, and covered it with the delicate reds and golds and greens. The buds trailed from each collarbone and the full pink petals of the two central blossoms encased the yellow stamen at the tips. The fabric of the dress came down from the shoulders at the sides and swept under them where they lay. It was neither frivolous nor ostentatious, she knew; it had contributed to her sense of modesty. And to have painted it! To have been able to see colors again, emerging like subdued drops of blood from her own skin. At the last moment she had taken the brush before the polished metal mirror and placed the tiny flutterings of birds. The birds of her own wisdom. It was almost as if she had taken flight herself. To see! To see! she thought. To take flight in the eternity of the present.

Teiresias's hair swung braided down her back, fell in a comforting knot at her waist. But Zeus was looking at her. And a flush rose up on both her cheeks. Still, she had always been uncomfortable with him. *Well—*, she thought, if this God touches me, I may have to throw my braid to Hera and climb up to save myself. It was well known that if Zeus took a fancy to a woman there would be no escape. She said, "Perhaps you are only saying that now—about beauty in women—now that I am changed. Let's continue our usual conferring. Let's not get off on an unfortunate tangent here."

"Why should I?" Zeus said. "It's not a tangent. It's merely a part. You're not old."

"No, that's true. My age seems to have diminished somewhat, but not too much fortunately."

"You're not silly either. I must say you have a tremendous vigor in this new form. I'm not trying to seduce you now," Zeus smiled. "I'm just admiring Hera's work. It's amazing how you remain the same as before and yet you are another sex. You were handsome as a young man, too, but I never really thought about it." And then he leaned over and held out his significant hand toward her breast. "May I touch you?"

"I don't think it's a good idea."

"All right," he said, "we'll think about it for a moment."

"Tell me something," Teiresias said. "What is it you look like when you're not with me, when you're not with humans?"

"Oh well, I guess I don't look much like anything. I never really thought about it. I guess you understand that—having been blind that is. I guess you of all people can know something without seeing it. Perhaps that's why you understand me better than most."

"Yes," Teiresias said. "But I began my life with sight. I always have an image."

A silence rested between them. Teiresias set her hands upon her knees and stared up at him. "You called me here for a reason, I suspect."

"Yes," Zeus said. "But I forget entirely what it is."

"Don't forget," Teiresias said. "I came to tell you something. But I forget it myself." There was a penetrating courtesy in her eyes.

"I do, too," Zeus said. "I forget the reason I sent for you entirely."

"I think I'll go home now then," Teiresias said.

"I think it's not a good idea," Zeus said. "We're alone now, let's rest a while with each other and think. Maybe we'll remember what we've come here to say. There is something about your eyes now," he said. "I can almost see your vision of the future right there in your eyes. I think you've been wrong. I think in the future I'm vividly alive."

"You know—" Teiresias said, standing up. Her skirts brushed uncomfortably against her feet. "I think it's a little cold in here. I think I will go along now. Call me when you have your questions; you know I will always help you out."

"Ah," Zeus said. "I remember it now. I have the idea for a birth. I want to call her Athena. Do I have to ask Hera about it? Hera is the Goddess of childbirth and marriage. Will I jeopardize anything if I give birth to Athena?"

"You already gave birth to Athena centuries ago. Why do you ask me these ridiculous questions? Athena is the Goddess of wisdom. She was not a real birth, she was just an idea that sprang out of your head. She is powerful, but you have not given birth. Hera has no hold on you over this. Even Hera will tell you it was not a real birth. Stop worrying."

"Teiresias?" Zeus said.

"No," Teiresias said.

"No?"

She looked into his terrifying eyes and saw all history laid out there. All maps of the past were there, and very little future. The rivers and valleys of desire were there.

"I don't think so," she said. She had all ready been with a man, had loved Emporous, lost him. It had been so long since she had been with a man. Centuries had passed, and now Hera had done it to her once again. Here she found herself again young, again with desires. To what purpose? she asked herself. What was this circling vision?

"Your lover has gone off to war," Zeus said. "A long time ago. You must be lonely now." Zeus did not say that no one had ever refused him. He didn't need to say that, he only had to look at her. She could see that it wasn't intimidation that had lent women to him.

"I don't know," Teiresias said. "You don't know how hard it's been," she said. "You don't know what it is to be human. I'm not used to being a woman. Here it is and then it's gone, and then here it is again. I've never gotten completely used to it. My mind doesn't change, it's the texture of my response."

"Sure you are, you're used to it," Zeus said. "It comes naturally to you. When you're a man, you want to be with someone. Why shouldn't it be the same for you now? You are all at once strong and wise and tender. It's very beautiful to see you like this. It's like looking at a rainbow. Come now," he said. "Let me take down your hair. Let me see all your beautiful hair around you."

"I don't really want to make this change—" Teiresias said, but in the end she realized that this time she hadn't managed to say it out loud. Not that he didn't know it without hearing it. But already he had begun. How had she gone so long without delicacy in her life? Once he had placed his hands around the sides of her face and put his mouth on hers, there was no stopping it, or wanting it to stop. Gently he untied the puzzle of her hair and smoothed it back from her face. His hands went down the back of her dress and then the front, and her clothing fell away, first the elegant dress that Teiresias had put on that morning, and then the underthings. She stood before him with only the painting on her breasts, fully sighted, her hands at the back of his head. Light! Light! It radiated from him. The warmth of light on his so-human body.

"Will you lie down with me?" he asked. "In full daylight? As one? With respect and self-confidence?"

"Yes," she said. "Only in that way."

"Are you sure?" he asked. "I won't take it from you."

"Yes," she said. "If you promise me one thing."

"I will," he said.

"Promise me you will never disappear. No matter what happens to Hera, you will always be there, if I need you. We will have continuity. It would be good for you to know this now."

"I promise you," he said.

"Do you promise?" she said. "Man or woman. God or not-God. Do you truly promise it?"

"I do," he said, and then he laughed. "It is one of my true promises. This one is true."

It is good to luxuriate in what we are. It is good to be delicate with someone.

The hands stroke down the body, make an offering. They would rescue Teiresias not from the knowledge itself, but from the pain of knowledge, from the misunderstanding and the envy that surround it, from the fear of inadequacy that all knowledge carries on itself. The hands go gently up and down the body again. The fear subsides now as differences part. The eyes are wide open, the world comes in, and the time is near. We know another's fear. Here, too, is desire.

As we rock this way, slowly we come to know ourselves. And slowly others help us; slowly we come to accept ourselves. Surely the hands are meaning. And slowly the meaning becomes a word in the life of emotion. Surely the body rises as man becomes woman becomes man again. Surely the meaning is the body rising.

Slowly the body opens itself for another, receives it with trembling, pity, compassion for oneself, for another cast lonely into this life, alone and hopeless. Cast into this life knowing that no other being knows what we have known. Knows what we have seen, done, been, will be, could be, will never be, will never know. Knowing that sometime at some point there is one who seems to know and understand that this is who we are, that this is who we can, will, are being, that there is someone who accepts us and we accept that one. How can we know comfort if we do not know discomfort? And how can this discomfort lead, as in all first things, to another smoother act, to the flow from one to another as the entry is soothed by oil, by words, by murmurings, by the gentle movement as the lips touch at the lips and neck. Words slip slowly in and out, as the wilderness beyond the town recedes, comes into focus. How do we rock this way without feeling something in the vast expanse we call our hearts? And a small red vehicle will come riding. Teiresias sees the dream again. A small red vehicle the color of the sun. And Teiresias does not know what it is.

V

The Birth of the World

In Boeotia, between the time when winter crystalizes the thoughts in one's bones and summer when the climate seethes and roils until the common man's madness is that of the unattuned dog, there comes a moment called spring. On the spur of just such a moment, Zeus entered into a blissful relationship with the daughter of Kadmos and Harmonia, sister of Ino, Agaue, Polydoros, and Autonoe. She was called Thyone, otherwise known as Semele.

Now Semele, a young and inexperienced woman, was especially excited by this large and bearded man. When he was in the throes of passion, it seemed to her, he changed his shape. When he was breathing gently beside her face, she would close her eyes tight and there on the backs of her lids she saw him: his tongue hanging out lovely and long and pink between his lower canine teeth, and over them: his nose drawn out narrow and black at the end, furred nearly to the tip. When he rubbed his face against her belly, it was an intricately feathered thing she saw: a dove perhaps. More than once he had amused her with his animal calls; and she, well—neither of them had ever been happier.

This was exactly what incensed the Goddess Hera: that Zeus, her mate, was with Semele in his human figure, something he had insisted he would reserve for the sight of the other Gods, no matter what the others might practice. "You are everything! You are everything to me!" Semele could be heard crying out—as far away as Mount Olympos. On the mountain the other Gods sighed to themselves and studied their feet. They could not look at Hera directly. Sitting in the Great Hall, they crossed their legs in front of the fire. It was as if the lovers' strange ululations had been amplified a thousand times.

When Hera had gone off to her own chambers, the other Gods said: Perhaps something astonishing is about to happen. For Zeus had never in the history of the world taken on so many forms with any one lover, certainly never a human one. So the Gods looked at their sandals when Hera came in to join them. There was Hera, the great Goddess of marriage and childbirth and agriculture, chewing on her fingers.

After what seemed to be years and at the same time only a matter of short moments, the other Gods quite suddenly found themselves leaning out from their couches. There below, beneath the coals of their comfortable fire, they saw what they in unison wished not to witness. First they saw Hera as they usually knew her: in her resplendence, her iridian hair flowing out around her ravishing face, her magical eyes. They heard her melodious voice gone angry, like a great bell ringing, while all the while she beamed up at them. "If the old mule can change forms every which way for his own advantage," Hera called out, "I can certainly use his hijinks—for all our benefits."

There she was: Hera at the door to Semele's compartments in the very ship that was carrying Semele's father, King Kadmos of Thebes of Greece as they knew him, along with the rest of the royal family, home from their travels in Egypt. Hera stood in the exact likeness of Semele's nurse: in the old woman's polished-apple face, with the two darting white eyebrows, the plump, very short figure in the slightly shorter purple robe. There was the old woman's voice in her throat. Only a God would have recognized her in the new miniature form.

Lithe Semele was stretched out on her adolescent stomach in the bedclothes, swinging her feet back and forth beneath the porthole. "Nanos," she said, seeing the old woman who was nearly short enough to have been considered abnormal, her mind on quite someone else. The sea was not very swollen that day, the waves not much of a problem. There was a pleasant sloshing in the background as if somewhere the Gods were drinking coffee.

"Semele, Semele," the Goddess of childbirth and marriage said warmly in the voice of another. There was an element of concern that was not entirely hard-hearted, for here was a young prospective mother in need of strong counsel. "Think harder, little Semele, about this." Hera in the form of the loving old nurse pleaded with her as only mothers and nurses can plead in such a situation. She placed her small hand like a starfish on the young girl's back and patted her as she had done from the girl's infancy. "Baby, baby," she said. "Don't hurt yourself."

"He is so good, Nanos."

"Yes," the old woman said, patting the girl on the shoulder with affection. "I know it. He makes you feel like a flower, I know it. But I have heard that very flower howling at night. What is it, Semele, makes a sweet thing like you into a howling of flowers?"

"Don't scowl at me, Nanos," said the innocent and affection-ate Semele, sitting up on the bed. She drew her little governess up with her, as often she did, and the tiny woman sat in her lap as if she had been one of Semele's most beloved stuffed play-things. "Please don't scowl at me," she said, for the relationship with her Nanos was more important to her even than that with her own mother. Semele lay her head on the shoulder of the petite governess she was holding.

"Hera will be displeased with you," the round woman said, brushing Semele's hair back where it had fallen out of the bar-rettes at the side of her face. She pinned the long black tresses. "Please be careful, little bunting. Hera's not someone to trifle with."

Suddenly petulant, she shrugged off her nurse's hand. "Hera has nothing to do with this," Semele said, and the old woman withdrew immediately, trundled down off the side of the bed to stand again at the knee of her young, royal charge.

"Hera will lead you when you bear a child. Then you will need not to have alienated her. There's still time to turn back, sweet innocent. Think what it means. He's Hera's husband."

"Nanos, please," Semele whined. "I know what I'm doing. Leave me alone, please."

The old woman tugged at the sleeve of Semele's nightgown. It was a gentle tug, the same as the old woman had been delivering since Semele learned her first words. To Semele it meant, You are going too far. "I am everything to him. Everything. And he is Zeus; he's chosen me, think what that means."

The old woman tapped at her sleeve. "He's been with others, many others."

"They didn't mean anything to him," Semele whimpered in an adolescent voice. "He told me. I am the only one who has ever meant a thing to him."

"Words. He has said it before. Certainly Hera has had more." The pitch on the boat had begun to smell again as it often did when the air was just so. And out the porthole window, standing now on the stool and looking out, away from her darling girl, the governess looked toward the eye of Ra painted on the blue bow. "Like a serving maiden, you eat only when others have eaten. You are only a small part of a pessoi game to him. If he saw someone else, or someone challenged him, or he just grew weary with himself—don't you see?"

"You've never believed in me," she cried out against her Nanos in the way of all young human beings. "You don't believe I could get someone extraordinary like that. There is no one above him. He chooses me and he is a God. A God chooses me, Nanos, he chooses me to be with."

"You are the only one who doesn't believe in yourself. That's why he preys on you, because you will think just what you have just said. You are going to ruin everything you have."

"You are jealous," the very young woman said. "You have never had a God for a lover and you are old."

"Zeus imagines he is the only one of importance," Hera said. "He grows more ludicrous day by day. Many think so, more and more."

"Stop it!" Semele cried, thrusting her hands to her ears. "Stop it! No one who isn't a fool can think unkindly of him. He is so hurt by the world, he told me so. He is so pained by it all."

"He says that to everyone, the best ploy of all. Poor sad manipulator of all."

"You don't even know how important he is to me. You have no way of knowing and you tell me what to do." Then Semele—involuntarily, certainly—glanced for just a second down at the front of her nightdress.

"You're pregnant now," Hera said. "Now you are pregnant."

Semele stared with her rich brown eyes at her Nanos, quite startled.

"Yes, I see," Hera said, turning cold in the old woman's frame. Yet there she stood again beside the bed where the young woman sat.

"Oh, Nanos, please don't be mad at me," Semele cried. "I'm to have a baby and I'm so excited about all of it."

But the old woman had pulled away from her. Nanos was shouting at her beloved Semele, and Semele was crying. "You, who have had less than half of everything Hera has had from that fool Zeus, will now have a child from him? Why don't you just ask him to come to you the way he came to Hera? Why don't you see how he will leave you behind when you ask, you and the little baby?" And then the old woman also was crying. She sat right down on the bed beside Semele and wept immense tears.

On the sixth of March, the sweet and silly—aren't we all a little silly at fourteen?—sumptuous, plump, and golden olive-skinned Semele, with black hair in tight spirals to her shoulder blades, sauntered out in a short tight skirt, two black spiders painted on her chest with all their hairy legs radiating round each taut breast, chewing betel nut, and singing lullabies to herself and to the son of Zeus, whom she had sworn was to bear the name of Dionysus.

"There's no objection here," the father of the universe said. "But why in the name of the Gods are you wearing a getup like that? You always seemed so sweet to me. Where are all your white bodices? What are these spiders on your chest and thighs? You've actually painted spiders on your thighs."

"Don't you like it, then?" she said, pert and challenging, leaning up against the oldest and most beautiful oak in the village of Thebes.

"Well, I don't know," he said, leaning toward her with his fingertips first, his lips following in a short quick sigh just beneath her ear. "It has a certain pull for me, a strange and perverse one that brings out something I've never known before. It makes me want to encompass you. Tell me, Semele-of-the-Spiders-Today, if I turned into the earth right now and opened myself, would you with all your crypt creatures fall inside me?"

"How just like you to say something like that," she said, chewing on her betel gum, all strident and annoying. "You know," she said, "I was never like this before I met you, you know that? Now I'm pregnant and I do funny things I never thought about before. I feel so content, and then I cry until I can't stop thinking. Then I cry for you wherever you are."

"I think of you when you're not there," Zeus said. "I think of you, too. I think of all the hilarious things you do. It makes me cheerful."

"Does it?" Semele said quite innocently. "Does it really?"

"Yes, of course. And I think of how delicious you are. And other things, you know."

"Like what? Tell me what you remember about me. Lately I've been feeling nonexistent, maybe it's part of being pregnant. You know the kind of things, when I wasn't so plump and lumpy."

"I think of you in your sandals," Zeus said. "The way you always like to wear your sandals—if ever your feet are going to touch the floor. I like it when your feet touch the floor," Zeus said. "And so I guess I remember the sandals."

"I was thinking lately I'd like sandals better if they weren't so flat. If they had sticks under the heels, then I wouldn't always have to be standing on my tiptoes. I get tired these days standing on my tiptoes."

"Yes," Zeus smiled, "I can understand that."

"What else do you remember about me when I'm not with you?" She had taken the long thin brush out of her bag and was dipping it into the black bottle. A spider spilled out of its tip onto her knee, and then she painted another.

"Why do you have to wear these spiders?" Zeus asked. "I really don't like these death cults."

"You don't need to like these death cults," Semele said, popping her gum emphatically, "since you know no death." Her curls bobbed up and down. "It's a kind of protest, if you'd look closely. It's not an embrace, if you see what I mean. Do you?"

"I'm trying," Zeus said. "But I'm not sure I like what I see. The change in you is very disturbing."

"Good," Semele said. "While you're disturbed, tell me what else you see in me, while I'm here within earshot."

"I like the way you chew the sheets when I touch you a certain way on your bottom."

"You do?" Semele said. "You like that? I never thought of you watching at that moment. I only thought of you doing. Tell me what else. I'm beginning to feel a little better. There are things going on here that are hurting my feelings. I'd rather think pleasant thoughts. Tell me what else you like about me. I never had anyone else; I don't know what it's like to see me."

"I like the way you are so plump," Zeus said, "and tender. Like a little chicken."

"A chicken?" Semele said in alarm. "I'm nothing like a chicken."

"Don't think so literally," Zeus said. "I'm not talking about feathers."

"You didn't like the feathers I brought you?" Semele said.

"I liked them all right," he said. "It was good."

147

"I thought you'd think them pretty," Semele said, sulking. "Peacock feathers are beautiful, I think. I thought you'd think them exciting. I had a hard time finding them."

"I liked them fine," Zeus said. "I liked other things better."

"Like what," she said, opening up her big eyes even wider.

"Like glacial encounters!" he laughed. "You look especially gorgeous in the snow," he said.

"And what else?"

"I don't know. You tell me then."

"I'll tell you what I remember best before we stopped for the sake of this baby."

"I don't want you losing it," he said.

"No, no," she said. "I know. Let me tell you this time. I like the silver hair on your chest, your big barrel chest," she said. "I like to call you Daddy. Oh Daddy."

Zeus laughed and sat down beside her.

"The way you wear your hair," she said. "The way it's so unruly. I like to yank it tight when I can't help myself, until I can see your jaw ache."

"You're way too brutal with me," he said. "I feel endangered."

"I like the way you sing," she said, "at certain moments. You know the moments?"

"Of course I do." He found he was actually tracing one of the hated spiders with his finger.

"I like how you go all shy and are sometimes unreliable."

"You do?" he asked, incredulous. "You like that?"

"Yes," she said, "I like it. I like the way you spring back. You always do spring back," she said confidently.

"I suppose so," he said. "I suppose I do with you."

"I like the way you moan," she said, "if I touch you just there on your back."

"I like the way you moan," he said back to her.

"Yes, but you moan very deep. It's like the whole sky goes black with the sound of it, and then I'm shaking."

"In terror," he said.

"No, silly, not in terror. I like the way you lose complete control of yourself if I touch you just there on your buttocks."

"I don't lose control of myself," he said.

"Yes, you do," she said. "It's completely reliable. I like the way you smell. I like the terrifying smell of your armpits." She laughed out loud and nuzzled up to him. "I like to bury my nose in your fur," she said. "All of it."

"You are a very naughty girl," he said.

"I am not," she said, suddenly indignant.

"I didn't mean that seriously," he said. "Really I didn't. Come now, why are you crying?"

"I'm not a naughty girl," she cried. "And I can't help crying. There's something hilarious inside of me, and all I can think of are birds and insects wiggling inside me. I don't know when I can stop crying sometimes. I'm not a naughty girl, don't you ever say it. You started it, you kept asking; you're the one who asked me again and again. If I'm naughty, then you're worse. You're more experienced."

"Yes, that's so," he said. "I'm very naughty myself. There's no denying it. Now why are you crying? I see no reason for you to be crying in the middle of such a fine list of our happinesses."

"You don't know how it is," she said. "My moods swing back and forth. One day it's insects I paint all over me, the next it's birds. Dead birds, horrible parrots with their heads cut off." Now she was truly crying, and he looked at her, alarmed.

"Semele?" Zeus said. "Is it really you acting like this?"

"Look," she said, "look at my thighs if you want to look."

"I see them. I think they're a little disturbing, Semele. I've never seen a girl with insects painted on her. I can't say I've ever seen a girl who painted more than the usual things on the usual areas. I find it deeply disturbing to see these insects crawling over you."

"I've drawn them crawling up like you used to do," she sniffed, "before I got pregnant. The insects crawl right in, like you used to do."

"Semele—" Zeus said. "I've been many things with you, but I've never been an insect."

"Before you, I had a future, and now I have nothing—"

"Of course you have a future," Zeus interrupted, all compassion. "You're going to have my baby."

"Now I have nothing but you, and I hardly ever see you. I have nothing at all. Now no one will speak to me. They think I knew before I did it with you— They think I knew. How was I to know? They say I am young and foolish and now I have ruined my life. Of course I am—young and foolish. I am young. I'm not even fifteen. And foolish. I am young, and foolishness comes of it, even I know that now. Now no one will speak to me. I can't even say good-day to my mother now. All day she cries, and my Nanos, even my Nanos, has gone away, frightened, she said, because of Hera. And all day a frog called baby jumps up and down inside and scares me out of my dreams. I'm frightened."

"Your eyes are wet with all this crying, you've got to stop now. What's happening to you? I can't believe you've painted spiders on your beautiful eyelids."

"This is my spider day," she cried out loud, sobbing into his chest as he put his arm around her. "All day I think of you without answer. Maybe today you will come even as a spider to me. Maybe you will wrap me in your web and drag me up the mountainside and eat my insides out. Disembowel me now, maybe it will happen today. Maybe, I think, he will even disembowel me."

"Don't be so morose, little one," Zeus said. "Don't go on like this at this time. You should be joyful."

"What do you expect?" she cried angrily. She threw her head back and shouted at him. "I know you're going to kill me. Everyone says I am stupid not to know that you were only lying. They think I knew it beforehand, but I didn't know. I believed in you. And now everyone tells me I am even more stupid because still I believe in you after the way you've left me alone all these days waiting."

"Semele, Semele," Zeus said.

"I may be stupid enough to let you be with me and to love

you, but now I know that you are a liar, everyone has said so, and they say that now you will kill me. You don't know what goes on here when you're gone, you don't know what it's like here—because of you. Everyone knows you will kill me, or your wife will. Everyone has already marked me dead. I should wreathe myself in vines and funeral perfumes—"

"Stop now, Semele," Zeus said. "Please stop this nonsense. No one's going to hurt you."

"Everyone says so, everyone says so. And they've already hurt me. I may be young and stupid, but I'm not ridiculous—or am I now?" And she started to cry again, this time uncontrollably. "I was a princess," she said. "My life was full and beautiful. There was nothing to stop my life. And now you have taken it away, even my mummy and my sisters won't speak to me." He pulled her up tight, but she shrugged him away. "Don't touch me," she cried. "It's all because of you. Because of you I paint these spiders. Tomorrow it will be worms crawling over me. And you won't even remember."

"Don't be so upset, Semele," Zeus said a little harshly. "You're worrying me now, the way you're talking. Worms will never devour you," Zeus said, ashamed of what he'd said to Teiresias. "I never meant to see you this way, my little darling."

"What did you expect?" she asked. "After what you've done to me. Everyone knows you're going to put me down. You've even sworn to kill me, the oracle at Delphi says it's true. You've even told Hera how you'll kill me."

Zeus sat stunned by the realization that his words had preceded him. To him it seemed increasingly ridiculous. He was increasingly conscious that others might come across them. "I was pretty," she went on, "now the maids won't even draw a bath for me. I was innocent, now the birds fly screaming away at the sight of me. When they set the table, they set no place for me. I eat on the floor with dogs now, because of what you've done to me."

"Please stop talking," Zeus said. "Please stop talking so much."

"Why should I stop?" Semele said, and when her eyelids came down he saw that she had bleeding spiders drawn on each of them. "Why should I stop when you are going to strike me down? Any human being would cry before you."

"I'm not going to strike you down," he said. "I'm going to straighten you out. I'm going to take the child out of you and let you go back to your old life."

"You're going to come to me like you came to her, that's what the oracle at Delphi said."

"I can't believe you," Zeus said, suddenly indignant. "What are you doing with that idiot oracle? Everyone knows she's a hoax. She causes trouble, that's all she does.

"Why did I do it?" he asked himself almost viciously. "Why did I ever get involved with this infernal mortal being?"

"You're going to come to me as lightning like you came to her. You're going to strike me down. You are, I know you are."

"Oh, please stop," Zeus said. "Please stop with all this non-sense now." And then she did something so childish that Zeus took in his breath with irritation. She reached up with her tiny fingers and took out her chewing gum, still sobbing, and stuck it to the side of the oak tree.

"Tell me it's not true. Tell me you're not going to strike me down," she yelled at him.

"I'm not," he said. "I'm not. Good grief, please stop."

"You are a liar, you are a liar," she screamed over and over again, until he rose up in great wrath uncontrollably and stared long and hard at her where she sat crumpled against the ancient tree. And in that moment, when again she called him a liar, when he had no intention of being one, in that moment, he struck her down before he could stop himself. With Hera's words ringing in his ears, "Kill her," and Teiresias's warnings ringing between them, "You can't kill the mother of your own child," he struck her down.

His lightning was said to penetrate the core of the gigantic tree, traveling down its towering length to impale itself in the ground just where she sat. And afterward there she lay, cut in two from top to bottom, one half of her face fallen to the one side along with the one breast, the one shoulder, and one arm, her tiny grasping hand, one hip, one half of her soft young bottom, one knee, one thigh, one tiny foot, all painted in fabric and in spiders. And the other side was just the same, fallen the other way. And the only thing not cut in twain was her womb, and out it fell like a nut from the oak itself, with the fetus in it, and rolled down the hill after him as he, Zeus himself, ran the other way. After him it rolled, and after him, until he turned to see what it was that followed him, and took it up in astonishment and even bereavement at what he'd done.

He stooped to pick it up and there it was, the little face staring out of the water drop. His son. With his fingernail he cut his own thigh then, deeply, and deposited it in his tissues. Then he seared it shut again. He felt it swimming then, little frog person in his leg, so near his bones. He hardly knew what to say to feel the other life swimming inside of him. And when he looked up at the hill he had left behind, a tower of flame had encompassed the tree. It rose up shining and stinking with the pungent scent of wood smoke as it would ever after on the Boeotian plains. And as history will tell you, a cult of young girls followed to this day after her, a cult of fire it was, named for Semele, the young girl who had briefly known Zeus and carried his son Dionysus, soon to be lord of the dance and the orgy, lord of the song and certain kinds of poetry. And ever after the young girls were said to worship at the burning tree, and ever after they were said to singe their lower parts closed, and ever after were virgins to her memory.

It seems so long ago, their fight. Yet they both remember it.

Zeus is pacing while Hera luxuriates in her bed. "So you're back," she says. "What was it this time? A caterpillar or a snake? A tufted titmouse?" She laughs, gathering speed. "Perhaps a naked mole rat? Was there a band of eagles singing overhead?"

She does not say that last night she saw him come in, his beard a hoary extravaganza of tangles, hair tousled to no end. His eyes were jet-black coals in his elegant head. She saw him dancing naked then in front of the polished metal mirror, saw the diffused image of him, smiling shyly back at himself only to disintegrate in a perplexed rage. If she had been younger, if he were still her brother and not her lover rejected and rejecting so many times over, she would have held his wild head against her chest, wrapped her hair around him, and cradled his sobs. How beautiful he was, his long limbs swaying before the reflection, his wide shoulders bearing up his portion of the sky.

"Zeus," she says. But she hears a voice.

"Zeus," it says. A taunt?

"Can't we—"

"Can't we—" It is a high-pitched mockery.

Zeus and Hera have shrugged each other off again. She dresses with the help of her maids and goes out to the courtyard. Her hair is braided down her back to give her air, the blue and green intertwined with indigo and violet. Each color makes a plait within the larger braid. They brush against the back of her ankles as she walks. It is so hot even here in the mountains that her peacocks wilt and drag their tails about like rugs, following after her. Down below: past the treeline of conifers, past the ragged rocky slopes where the flatter lands begin, are there not usually the light green tufts of olive trees, the snaggled dark green vines of grapes? It would only take a little effort, Zeus. Where is the rain? The plains are smoldering. Zeus is arguing. And she: what of her pomegranate and apple trees? She will inspire someone to carry water from the stream.

"Women have it better than men in sex," Zeus chides, coming up behind her.

"That is the only thing you haven't managed to turn yourself into, isn't it?"

"I wouldn't degrade myself," Zeus says.

"You wouldn't *degrade* yourself? You who have been a slug wouldn't *degrade* yourself? You, Mr. Thunder, Mr. Rain. Pretty soon the fact that men have a zealous time in sex and women don't will hardly mean a thing."

"Women have every pleasantry. Pampered from morning to night without a pain."

"Is that so?" Hera smiles. "Perhaps you should have a child."

"Perhaps I will."

"That's not bloody likely, now is it? Even for you."

Teiresias is rubbing the astonishment from his eyes with his fists. The Gods have called him in to settle an argument, he who even at his young age has reportedly traveled through time, through space, through madness and sanity, through the sensibilities of both sexes and all their sorrows and joys. Zeus puts the question to him: "Who has more pleasure in sex? Who receives the most—man or woman—Teiresias?"

"Yes," Hera says softly. "Tell us, Teiresias, we hear that you've had a dream, and in it you were everything."

Teiresias and Emporous are taking the air, strolling through the evening on the eve of Kadmos's return. "What can we expect?" Teiresias asks. "What will become of Polydoros when he is just a man again, son of the king?"

"Not just a man, he was never just a man," Emporous says, beating back the leaves with a stick as they pass under a low-hanging tree.

"Yes," Teiresias says. "Yes, never a man. Never a God, never really a king."

Emporous raises his brow.

"It will be a splendid night for looking at the Gods," Teiresias says. "When the orange light has taken the yellow away, and the rose the orange, and the violet the red, and the white pierces only minutely the black—"

"Yes," Emporous laughs, "we have just got time for all that."

How far they have come from those first days together when everything lit them on fire. Now one moves next to the other in a slow constant burn, like two stars circling one another, two pinpricks in the sky. He says so, and Emporous smiles.

"If you look hard enough you can see the two of them together," Emporous says. "Or—" he laughs, "am I going blind?"

Teiresias strikes him on the shoulder. "Don't say such things."

"Last night I heard the rumblings of Athena, I thought of my mother then, and then naturally I thought of war, of the rumors, of Kadmos coming home."

Emporous clasped his young lover's, the developing seer's, arm. "Have you seen his return—Kadmos's return? Have you foreseen it at all?"

Teiresias frowned. "Only the ship coming in, only the messengers going out."

The events of that year gathered momentous volition from the first day of spring until the last day of the hard season when the ship fifteen miles away pulled into sacred Delium. It carried the great beast that had been sent for by Polydoros; and it bore King Kadmos himself, Harmonia the queen, and their daughters, sisters of the youthful momentary king, Teiresias's good friend, Polydoros. The giant hippo was herded down the plank into the red dust of the street. Children ran this way and that, afraid and curious. Even grown men ran at the sight of it. All the way from Egypt the animal had been shipped to prove to Ameinius that he, Ameinius, had worth. Far too late. All men had it, worth and the right to live a peaceable life. Polydoros had proved it. Here was the sign. Larger than a one-story house, grayer than a winter day, with pink inner nostrils and breath hot as August that cast its few inner hairs, like wires, about in the torrent, each foot the size of a wine cask, and importance etched into its hide. Down the narrow street it ran, like a thunderstorm bellowing across the plains. Yes, the sign had arrived. *Hippopotamos.* Yet Ameinius the assignee had died. King Kadmos had arrived.

Teiresias recalls it for Hera and Zeus: his flight into a fantastical land where chariots ran without horses and buildings stood like mountains on end. There Thebes was only a fanciful story, repeated now and then. But the Gods would hear of his transformation instead, how he was swept into another body, her shoulders white and creamy as the owl's milk, so his mother had called it, that flowed from her breasts whenever thoughts of Athena filled her head.

Perhaps he had caught the experience from his mother, this set of overlapping occurrences. Perhaps there was nothing unusual at all in his experiences and the way he remembered his own tender new breasts, pale there between his arms. The moment itself a confusion of incident never to be untangled, the product never to be forgotten as long as Teiresias lived. That moment when he was both, seen and seeing, woman and man. Two male eyes looked at him, glistening like agates. Turn around and turn around again. Far down under the clapboard housings of his ribs a warmth reared up—Teiresias!—seemed to be tucked up, concentrated now into a burning in the pulp of him that radiated out, out, and away, down the insides of his legs. Then it was as if his sex had been turned inside out. Something fitted itself tightly inside.

Who knew how the realities coincided—which was the polished wood, which the inlaid? Vertigo—he saw the woman, dark hair full out around the high bones of her face and the slope of her shoulders, luminous, until—vertigo—he saw his own feminine face looking up from between new arms. And—turn about once again—there a dark masculine face, strong at the jaw, the meaty shoulders, a chest broad and covered with softly curling hairs that invited the cheeks and lips, and under the fingertips the long gentle curve of the back. He had never quite seen it this way. Then the pounding, now powerful, now

157

gentle, driving into that part which Teiresias as a woman came intimately to understand.

Emporous, alarmed, laid his arm around Teiresias's shoulder. "Athena is beating for war then? Is that it, Teiresias? Are we all to go then?"

"The Would-Be King is beating for war. He has trumped it all up for Kadmos's return. A way to get his men their promised glory."

Emporous sat down at the crest of the hill overlooking the town, the valley far below, and put his head in his hands.

"We will go together."

"Of course."

"Isn't that something anyway, Emporous?"

"We'll be lost from one another. Is it true? Can you see it? Will we be lost from one another?"

"I see nothing," Teiresias said. "I see nothing of the details. You've been to war, what does it mean?"

"It means living death. It is the worst of all your possible imaginings. Only the exhilaration of hope will pull you through."

"But I haven't told you—"

"What is it? For the sake of sanity let me have it now."

Teiresias wrung his hands. Sitting there on the cliff of the small hill, looking out, to him it was as if the purple mountains all around the great plain held him for a moment with his friend in Greece's cupped palm. "We're not going together," he faltered. "All the other men and their favorites will march out together. All of them except for us. You have to go alone. I saw it last night. You walked down the road with the spiked cap of the hedgehog on your head. I fell down in the road and wept."

"We *will* go together," Emporous bellowed in front of him, shaking him by the shoulders so angrily Teiresias felt his neck would snap. "It's a lie," Emporous yelled into his face. "No one goes to war without his favorite. How can anyone keep up his strength without the love of his friend? Without his good friend to protect? He would fall down and die alone and be eaten by dogs." His fierce eyes stared into Teiresias's own while he clasped his hand around Teiresias's upper arm like a metal arm-band for war. "I will not leave you to pine at home, no matter who orders it; I will not go by myself."

"Sometimes I don't understand my own dreams. Perhaps I'm wrong, very wrong." The two of them sat down together heavily at the crest of the hill. "What rubble!" Teiresias said. "What city once lay here?" He kicked at a stone with his foot. Down the slope it swept, gathering its own speed.

"You *are* wrong," Emporous shouted. "How long can I live with these obscure futures tattooed to our chests? Why can't you get that straight? You are viciously, cruelly wrong to talk this way when you're not sure."

"Yes," Teiresias whispered. A bronze moon was rising up over the horizon in the afternoon sky. A complete and pure cir-cle, uncut. He ran his hand over Emporous's heavily muscled back, memorizing him with his fingertips, the thick flesh, the radiant warmth that carried Emporous's own pungent smell.

"I won't go alone," Emporous said bitterly.

"I won't let you go alone, I'm coming along. It was foolish-ness. We're going together—when the time comes. Soon we will go together to fight."

Emporous's head went into his hands; and the back of his neck, his spine, the back of his rib cage, all of him shook as he sobbed.

"I'm wrong, I must have been wrong," Teiresias cried out, afraid at the sight. "I've been wrong before."

"When?!" Emporous bawled into his hands. He thrust his head up from his arms. "When were you wrong?"

"Yes!" Teiresias exclaimed, casting desperately for a thought. "I was wrong about the green hat. It never came true. We have no idea what it meant."

"Insignificance!" Emporous sobbed, his voice broken in half. "What's in a green hat?"

"Wait! Please wait!" Teiresias clapped his dearest friend

repeatedly on the back. "There was one other time. It was the red chariot. I never understood that."

"Stop it!" Emporous yelled. "Stop it! Not understanding means nothing. Nothing, I tell you. I have been in a war. I have been in it, I say. I know what *that* means. To go alone! Do you know what *that* means? And you, what will happen to you? Why won't you be able to go? What in the name of the Gods is about to happen to you? Tell me—stop holding back. Tell me! It would be easier than this half-light we are always living in."

What was there to say? He knew nothing more. First a deadly resignation overcame him, a depression of spirit and will, and then a fury began almost at once to grow in his limbs, moving closer and closer to the center where all of a sudden he could not control himself at all. "I am going!" he shouted toward the skies. "No matter what! Take this curse from me!" he cried. "I will go like a man with my friend."

Then he saw a small thing that at some other time might have been a thing of beauty to him. There in the grass, like two braids of a rope, were two snakes coupling, undulating as if in the world there was no such thing as parting, as death or overwhelming pain.

"In the name of Zeus," Teiresias cried, "look at that! Mating when we are to be driven like animals into separate holes. Perhaps to die. Look at the wretched things!" With that he took a stick and flung it directly at them. For a moment in the twilight it was hard to tell which of the three objects in the air was the stick, but when they came down, two darted in opposite directions, and the other lay broken, as if blind, at Emporous's feet.

"My God," Emporous said aghast. He stood up and moved slightly away. "You have broken their love, you have broken a sacred act."

"Ours is to be broken," Teiresias spat. "We do not even know why."

Then he saw in Emporous's face an astonishment he had never before seen. "What is it?" Teiresias asked in a panic, staring down at himself in search of something to account for

Emporous's wonder and horror and glee—perhaps some spectacular gift from the Gods resting upon himself, some raiment of gold, a talisman perhaps strung around his neck, a cut in his leg, a spectacular insect, he didn't know what.

Emporous's hand reached out toward him, very cautiously, as if Teiresias might disintegrate at his touch, and Emporous with his fingertips stroked just once the line from Teiresias's newly formed face, to the breasts Teiresias was seeing for the first time blooming above her waist, to the dewy inlet, and beyond to the peculiarly small and trembling feet. "Now they will never let you go with me, I will never be able to go with you."

Emporous wept in their fantastic new embrace.

Somewhere deep inside the bowels of the earth, a fissure had begun to open itself. Fishing boats cast about in reckless seas. Vases trembled on tables and in the granaries. But what had she done, Hera worried. After all, she had had Semele destroyed— a young woman, alone and bereft—even before her child's birth. Had she no duty to Semele, and to her child? Hera agonized. This had not been the act of the Goddess of childbirth, the work she loved; it was the act, Hera knew, of the vehement and miserably betrayed.

Yes, it was not her feelings for Zeus that bothered her in this; it was the act of maternity that mattered to her. It was the visage of a child's minuscule face blossoming from seed, burning gently in the womb toward life. It was the nurturing of the belly and its warmth, the blue milk spilling from each woman's breast, the baby's face pressing between the lips between the legs, it was the sacrifice in pain for life and growth and nurturance.

And she knew she did not care for Zeus, and now Zeus wanted to bear the woman's child. It was all too like him to think that he could encompass it. Surely it would change him some. Once Zeus had carried another life in his own body and afterward had looked into the newborn baby's eyes, once he had felt the sweet unworldly breath he had given it brushing upon his own cheeks and lips, once he had taken in the untouched breath of his child into his own nostrils, all masquerade—for a moment at least with him—would disappear. All mothers had had that trembling, naked joy.

And who would this child, born not of Semele, born of no intimate part, become? A thigh was only a thigh, after all. Teiresias had told her this: the child would be Dionysus, God of the orgy, of the third leg. But also, the child would be the father of music and poetry, so Teiresias had said—if one could believe in her/him. And he would love his mother, eternally—his own mother, lost Semele. And wine, Teiresias had said, the child would be the God of wine. He would not be like Zeus's only other offspring, Athena, born fully grown from a thought, without pain or love or woman's delivery, to be the Goddess not only of wisdom but of the rationale for war, which she disdained.

Then Hera smiled to herself for the first time in a very long while. Yes, she thought, I will do this to save the child for its mother's sake and for my own integrity. I will do it for the child, as I have always done for anyone's child. Zeus could do as he pleased. Yes, he had no idea what it was like; the wrenching certainty of life and death as an infant came out in blood from between your knees. And if I do this for him, she thought—for he could surely not accomplish it alone—he will have to acknowledge me for what I am. He will never be able to forget that I have guided him. He will have to acknowledge what I know—even if I should someday choose to abandon him because of everything he has done.

It was as if a stone had been thrown into a pond—he was the pond—the moment he first felt the baby moving. Until then he had felt a certain fizzing in his inner thigh, as if the Spring of

Tilphussa had been turned loose there. He had felt, he thought, as Teiresias had said, a certain cell division. But then it was as if a stone had been cast into his leg and he felt it falling. The hollow sound of it washed inside him as though he were the banks and water and floor. He had been mammals, yes, birds and reptiles, humans, raindrops, fire and lightning, sound, but never this. He scratched his thigh thoughtfully and went about his daily walks, ambling rather inconspicuously he thought.

It went easily for a time, aside from a slight round of nausea upon early-morning wakings. Hera had been unmistakably kind to him lately. And he to her, certainly. They were like a newly expectant couple. The tender looks and kisses, Hera's hand laid upon his inner thigh at all odd moments, there to detect the most subtle of movements. She swore shortly after they had made love one morning that she could feel the baby smiling. There!—she said—was the slight upturning of the infant lips and there! the crinkling at its eyelids. She thought she felt the birth waters shaking with a certain mirthfulness.

One morning while walking in his sandals, a bit laboriously—it was noticed by other Gods looking out from their individual breakfasts—Zeus sat down suddenly and lifted his foot up before him. In their sandal, his great toe and his second toe had been greatly altered. Slightly swollen and pinkish, both toes had fallen over in opposite directions. There seemed to be no point of disconnection, yet there they were in this painless contortion. It was as if they had swung open like a door on its leather hinges.

Near the central fountain, his ankle across his other knee as he stared down at himself, he for the first time made out the outline of an entirely other person curled inside his own leg. Until that moment it had been merely an idea. Now the infant had begun to take on an existence of its own. For the first time Zeus realized that the world was not an extension of his own imagination. My God, he said, uncharacteristically, slapping his hand in dismay against his brow. "Hera!" he shouted; "Hera!" he shouted. "Hera! Come now!"

"What is it? Are you all right?"

"Look what's happened!" he cried, pointing at his foot. "I can barely walk. And look!" His voice fell into an awestruck hush. "Look, Hera!" There just at the bottom of the hem of his short toga, curled on its side, was the outline of the fetus, its little bottom, spine, and skull. "There it is—"

"Oh my," she said. "Look at it sleeping, and see there, Zeus—it's sucking its fist."

"No. Yes, it is!"

"It's a good-sized one," Hera said. "You're doing very well."

"Yes," he said, still staring at his thigh.

"*Very* well."

"But Hera," Zeus said, "how will it get out?"

"All mothers say that at one time or another. By the looks of your foot," she said, pointing at the separation of joints in his two toes, "that is the place." Together they stared at it, the slightly swollen skin.

"With Athena, Hera," he said, "I imagined her and in that instant there she was: sprung into your arms—from a thought. But this—this is something entirely else."

"There now," Hera smiled, rubbing his shoulder. "You've just begun. Your joints are loosening. When I was pregnant—all three times—out grew my belly so large that my navel stuck straight out like a thumb."

"That's a lie," Zeus laughed. "Don't tease me like that."

"It's not," Hera said. "It's certainly not."

"That's a bald-faced lie if I ever heard one. You don't even have a navel."

"I did when I was pregnant."

"No."

"Yes indeed, I took on a completely human form."

"I don't remember that you had a navel."

"At first it was absolutely as I'd expected. But then my hips swung open wide at the pelvis—just like a door. I started to waddle and my navel stuck straight out like a thumb."

Suddenly in front of them then, the fetus that had been lying with its head nearly up to Zeus's groin turned upside down. "Oh thank goodness," Hera said, "its face is toward your bone. It will be an easy birth."

"An easy birth?" Zeus said.

"Yes, yes, quick and easy."

"Why must its face be toward my thigh bone?"

"Otherwise the hard back of its head is against the bone— much more painful. This is good, rest easy, you're doing beauti- fully." And they made love with Zeus sitting on the steps to the fountain and Hera between his now very different legs. It was just as Hera had said—Semele was a completely forgotten thing.

The sway of his back as he walked became more and more marked as he tried to support the baby on one side. Then walking became impossible as the baby began to encroach on his knee. Not only his leg swelled, but his whole body seemed to have been blown up. During the night he took on addition- al bloat until it felt as if every inch of him had stretched tight; his cheekbones were nowhere to be seen. His beard resembled a piece of goat's wool glued to a bowl with two slits painted for eyes and a flat monstrous thing stuck on for a nose. His face had lost all Godly definition. The same was true for his neck and his arms: his torso was worse, if that was possible. Zeus felt like an urn with a tippy bottom. He was miserable: he had never been known as pudgy in his life. And now there was no escape—not into any person or thing. He had sworn to see this through without distraction. He would be what he would become, and he would deliver what would be. Inside of his own being was another, growing most rapidly—today tiny fingers, tomorrow the thin translucent lids for the eyes. Fol- lowing that, the eyes would open, peering about in the dark. Perhaps the light would flow in from the room through the layers of his thigh, through ichor and tissue in some muted reassuring way. He wanted most to be reassuring to this new being who would come into the world innocent of what could be done to one, of what could come of innocent action and delay.

"Teiresias," Zeus said, "I've got myself into a fix."

"I'm not surprised," Teiresias said.

"What do you mean?"

"Kill her," Hera said. "You promised me you would come to her the same way you came to me, as lightning. It will kill her," Hera laughed. She doubled over. She was beside herself. "You promised, and you always keep a promise. It's the one thing I can always count on with you."

*

"You can't kill her," Teiresias said to Zeus. "How can you be a loving God if you kill the human mother of your own child?"

"The God you described killed his own son. I will keep the son. Besides, I promised Hera."

"There you go using human beings for your own purposes again. You have to use them for the good of someone else. That's exactly what I warned you against. You must love her very much."

"Yes, I love the little girl."

"I meant Hera. You must truly love Hera in order for you to kill the young woman you love so much, when she is carrying your baby."

"No, it's horrible," he said with disgust.

"You don't have to say these things to me."

"No," he said, "I wouldn't. It's truly horrible."

"Don't stand on form with me, it's not necessary. You've promised Hera a lot of things and you haven't kept your word. Why do you acquiesce now? In this?"

"Think straight. It's simple, isn't it? Hera rules marriage and childbirth. If I don't acquiesce, Hera will kill her anyway. She's already cut her off from all her friends and family. Semele lives in utter silence. No one will speak to her—even strangers won't speak to her in the marketplace. The day Hera discovered Semele with me, Semele was dead in Thebes. She's for all practical purposes already dead. She lives like one with the devouring disease. I might as well do it myself. And—" He cocked his eyebrow mischievously. "I will save the child."

"You will save the unborn child?!"

"Wait and see. I will make an everlasting God out of me, and my son. Wait and see."

And so the woman he most despised told him to do it, and so he said he would. It was a matter of honor with him to do as he had said he would, in some cases. It was hard to say what controlled him. The tenderness and innocence of the girl he had loved made no difference in the face of Hera's force. Besides, it was convenient. And the girl, it was true, was silliness itself. Even though her skin was a lovely olive silkiness, her eyes mahogany and sparkling, and she was sumptuous and plump, she echoed everything he said. She could not hold her tongue; whatever she heard she said, no matter where or to whom. "Well," he said to Teiresias the man. "She is silly."

"She's still an innocent. You should have thought before you got into it with her. She looks smart but she's not. She even seems brilliant at first. But at the first touch of intimacy she reflects whatever you say. She cooks, that's all she can do. She's like a windup princess who cooks and entertains the local guests. She's calculating, and she's a reflector, that's all she is. She will swing whichever way will make her more popular."

"Like Echo," Zeus said.

"No, not like Echo," Teiresias said. "You've missed the point again. Echo was intelligent."

"No," he said, pondering. "I think being with Hera is even better than being with Semele, considering how silly and dangerous Semele is."

"I never said that Semele was more dangerous than Hera is."
It was true that Hera controlled many factors in his life. He, Zeus, was a mere string, he said to himself, and Hera had a hold on one end of it, sometimes both ends, he thought. And then see how he jumped. He gave her everything she wanted, beautiful things, to try to stop her viciousness, but to no avail. He did not know that he could not give her what she wanted. It wasn't in him to do so. She wanted someone else, someone entirely else, and she had others secretly in mind. And so Zeus had no direction of his own for the moment, though his power was significant. The winds raged across the hills and mountainsides; sheet lightning blazed the iridescent dark without result. Nowhere was there rain. And everywhere there rose up criticism of small kings, as whole populations began breaking down in turmoil and disease.

This was an impasse between former lovers that was understood by Teiresias, as were many impasses understood by such a seer. He understood it because it was not an uncommon human or Godlike thing to be caught up in something he called The Web of Attachment Without Vision. The Web of Attachment Without Vision was the descent into hell. And Teiresias could see its circumstance without ever having to have lived it in his own bones. The web Zeus and Hera knew was a darkness even greater than any darkness Teiresias had known.

"Well," Teiresias said, a bit uncomfortably. "I forgot to tell you something. I forgot to tell you about the virgin birth."

"You forgot to tell me about the virgin birth? What is the virgin birth?"

"Well, its an important part of it. I would have told you, but you're always rushing off. I can't think in such short spurts, and then there's no way to contact you when I think of anything. I'm not a sprinter. I'm a long-distance runner," Teiresias said. "I'm not a drop in your bucket, if you see what I mean."

"Stop stammering," Zeus said, "and tell me what it means."

"I'm not sure what it means," Teiresias said.

"Come on, man," Zeus said, "stop dickering."

"It has something to do with purity. The child of the God must have a certain purity."

"Semele was a virgin, I'm sure of it."

"Yes, but she's not now."

"That's the one thing you've said I'm sure is true. Why would anyone want a virgin to give birth? I mean it's not impossible certainly, but why?"

"I can only take a guess," Teiresias said. "I don't think it's because a woman who isn't a virgin is impure. That would seem to be the case on the face of it. But I don't think it's that.

"I think it's because the child must be born of an untouched spirit. It has to be entirely new. It can't be the descendant of anything, or it's not the beginning of, well—creation, so to speak. It doesn't wipe out anything that went before."

"Good grief, man," Zeus said, "try to make some sense. Why would anyone want to wipe out what is already there?"

"Because it doesn't work," Teiresias said. "That is the source of all change. It's extraordinarily easy if you'd just let it sink in. It's very simple. Because it doesn't work. That's all."

"Good grief," Zeus said. "I think you're going mad, dreaming up these things. If I didn't know you better, I'd think you made it all up to torment me."

"I can think of others more likely to do that for you."

"Yes," Zeus said. "I see that anyway. I see that part of what you say. I don't understand any of the rest of it. Tell me about this all-consuming God. What is impermanence anyway?"

The very last of his pregnancy did not go along quite as pleasantly as he had anticipated, though, as Hera said, there was nothing disastrous, nothing even abnormal or worrisome about it. It bothered him so much he did not even wish to think about it even as it was happening. "My God, what is it!" he cried. "What if it turns out to be a hyena trapped inside, laughing at me?" he said one moment. And then the next: "Oh, the splendid little rabbit is nibbling at my insides—pretty little girl or a boy, it might be either one—" And even Zeus, a God, had to wait, having failed to look in that moment when he plucked the babe from its poor dead mother and plunged it into his own thigh.

Not until the waters of labor gushed out of his foot did he allow himself a moment to think about the most recent experiences of his pregnancy, and then only as a kind of relief for his fright at what was taking place. He was lying in bed with his foot propped on a pillow, the foot itself over the edge of the mattress, when the water broke. Out between large toe and second, through the tiny slit no bigger than two inches, came a flood of hot water. Out onto the floor it sprang like a hot shower, in a cascade. The sound of it was as if whole buckets had been poured through his leg.

"It's coming!" he shouted. "The baby, the baby—it's coming out!"

Hera, mother of earth and childbirth, did not stand away from him. "Don't worry," she said. "It's only your water breaking. Tell me exactly when the first pain begins. It might not be until morning."

It was as if he had become a chicken again, thinking only of his own long, skinny, lightly feathered neck, rooster for a night. Beautifully feathered in rust and green with a great red piece of flesh on the top of his head that took an exhilarating leap every time he strutted up close to a hen. When it filled with the sacred ichor of a God turned animal for the night, he let loose a crow that ripped fault lines through the deep continental shelf of a wild distant land. His mind was filled with these dreams. It was his unfortunate departure from the barnyard that came full force into his mind as his labor began. He remembered the moment when he had let himself be so distracted that two immense human hands managed to take hold of his scrawny feathered neck. Between chest and chin, completely around, front and back, they had gripped him tight as a tinker's vice. By the neck! Without any concern for his feelings, they had begun to wring and squeeze everything he cared about to death. Only sudden thundershowers had saved him in the end. His human assailant lay in the dirt of the yard small and crisp as a fried egg, surrounded by hens.

The latest wretched moment before his lightning-bolt escape seemed now to be revisited upon his thigh. Here was the first pain of birth, and already he looked to see whether his leg had gone purple with bruises. Already he moaned audibly. How could anyone squeeze any harder? Hera placed a warm towel on his leg. "There, there," she soothed. "Keep your spirits up. Now you've had a taste." She smiled right into his eyes. "Soon we'll see the little sprout that even I have come to love. Yes, tomorrow—or the next day, no doubt. Take care to pace yourself."

Zeus nodded powerfully and leaned back in his bed as the maids came in to towel up the waters he had expelled. For one moment the shimmering pool lay on the floor, and then in the next the women were sponging it up. It had gone. Zeus said to himself sentimentally, my baby swam there—for how long? No one, not God or human being, wanted to remember how long.

Toward the end Zeus had been so fierce one moment, so gentle another, what with the turning little beast, as he called it in his irritable moments, inside of him biting and pinching and kicking and then stroking his emotions so tenderly. Just the night before, the baby must have stuck its hand up into his groin, or perhaps its head or foot. Yes, that's the way it was by now, of course, so Hera had told him. It was still feet up. It is still feet up, he repeated to himself, the sweat breaking out on his brow. He swore he had felt it turn around several times since it had first planted its head by his knee, kicking all the while. Yes, its head was turned face in toward the bone. "An easy birth, quick and easy, and then you will see your baby's face."

"Yes," he sighed dreamily, with an imagine of the baby before him, and he fell asleep while Hera stroked his face with a cold towel.

The day Zeus gave birth to Dionysus, the whole world

shook, the great oceans parted, melted rock poured from the earth. Sands shifted horizontally, and buildings and bridges collapsed. Dams and water mains burst while sand and mud sprang in floods from giant cracks in the earth. Continents broke apart and were set adrift. Everywhere large and even small bells were shaking and ringing clamorously. And for Zeus how was it? Throughout all the ups and downs, the contractions and rests, it seemed as if the peoples of the earth were going at each other in his thigh. A fire burned. Whole populations rushed one way, then the next.

"Excruciation!" he yelped repeatedly. The environment quaked. Down his leg and out his foot between the large toe and the second one, the child had begun to come. Zeus agonized so dreadfully it was said he ground his teeth together until he chipped a tooth.

"There, there now," Hera comforted, "it could be much worse. This is so much easier."

"The easy way?!" he yowled. "I'm carrying a baby—in my leg."

"Yes," she whispered fondly, wiping the tears like rain from his cheeks. "It could be coming out somewhere else—"

"What could be worse! The thing is coming out my foot."

"He could come out your most tender part instead," Hera ventured. "That's the way others have always done it. It could have gone the other way. It could have come out of your sex instead. A woman's sex is no less tender than yours."

Zeus looked down at his mammoth leg, his foot swollen as a womb might have done. It was ten times its normal size, with the head of the infant butting against the ball of his foot, pushing toward the swollen opening between his large toe and the next. He looked then at the small bewildered penis curled against his other thigh. "My God," he said. "It could be worse."

"I didn't know you had a God," Hera smiled. "But it's all right." She covered his brow with kisses and stroked his temples, one and then the other, as he lay back to rest.

"It's happening again!" he cried. "Here it comes again. What if I die?"

At this Hera laughed and rubbed his shoulder blades where he was curled over his own legs, his disparate feet straight out before him. "Now, now, love. You're not going to die. It's a common fear, but you are not going to die."

"I *am* dying. I've taken on too much this time. I made a promise I can't get out of, and now I'm going to die. And the little one, the little one—what if the little one dies too? Please take the little one, Hera, if I should die." Great racking tears fell out of his eyes and swept down the mountainside through the drought-ridden valleys, wiping out villages large and small along the way. When they reached the sea, a great tidal wave sprang up and rocked its way over every country that had a coastline, and some nearby and inland. "Please keep her," he said. "Or him—the little one."

"Of course, of course," Hera said, and she kissed him on the mouth. "You're not going to die, my love. I promise it."

With the next contraction, his foot nearly threw itself off the bed of its own accord, his whole body writhing after it. The four smaller toes bent one way and his great toe bent the other. When it was over, he gasped: "How do you know, how do you? How can you say it? I am dying, I tell you."

"There!" Hera shouted, probing his foot most painfully. "There I see the hair!" she cried.

"I'm dying, I'm dying!" he cried. "Get it out of me, please get it out. Cut off my foot! Cut it off!"

"You're not dying!" Hera said. "Everyone always thinks that."

"Dying!" he screamed, and Australia broke away and drifted southward on a great wave. "Some women do die! Others have died doing this."

"I promise you anyway, you're not dying," she said. "Keep faith."

"Keep faith," he dozed, dreaming then. "Keep faith." A

whole dream of animals floated before him, all clucking and mewing and swimming in thunder and rain.

"Arrrgh!" he cried, and he woke suddenly. "No, I can't let it happen again. I'm going to change," he screamed. "I'm going to change into someone else, into something."

"It's too late for that." Hera massaged the ankle bone where the infant still lay curled: its bottom there, the back of its head bulging like a large gourd in his arch. "You're lucky," she said, "you're lucky its face is against your bone rather than the back of its head. And," she said, "it's right side up, head down. An easy delivery. Keep thinking that: an easy delivery. You're doing very well."

"My God," he cried, and she just smiled. "My God, I'm going to throw up."

"Lean over," she said, "and let it come. Let it come now, don't hold back. I'll put a cold cloth on the back of your neck."

Out it came and out it came, fiery and hot, flowing down the mountainside and out to sea. Down along the bottom of the ocean it ran, there to spring up again and again, dotting the water with boiling spots of molten rock hundreds of miles across.

"You'll feel a little better now," Hera said. "Now the hard part starts."

Nothing came out of him but a breath then, long and moaning and low. He closed his eyes and stared at the insides of his lids.

"Keep thinking it," she said. "A quick and easy birth. And it will come very soon."

Anyone could have seen that he had gotten very pale.

"Breathe deeply now: in and hold. Now push," she said. "Push like a God."

"I'm dead soon," Zeus said.

"Stop it," she said. "Gods don't die. Don't give out on us now."

"It could go on for eternity—Hera! Hera! Help me. It might never stop. That could happen to me. I've made a horrible mistake—think of what's his name rolling that rock up the hill over and over again, or what's his name getting his liver eaten out by a bird. And I caused some of that. That was what I did."

"Stop it," she said, "and pay attention. We need all your attention now."

"I've gone too far. I'm the first male God to give birth and I'll be the first God to really die. I can't do this! I can't do it! It takes over my whole mind."

"That's good," she said. "Show a little concentration. That's good. It won't be long now. Cooperate, don't lose hope, push for goodness sake."

All the muscles up and down his calf began to writhe like the boa constrictors he'd imported for amusement from warmer climates. "It's death," he bellowed, "growing in my leg."

"Stop it," she said. "Be strong, it's only your leg."

"*Not* just my leg," he said, holding his breath until he was nearly a sunset. Radiant particles showered water and earth. "It takes me over. Over, I say. I'll change all my ways, Hera. Don't let me die."

"It's not your torso for goodness sake. If we can't get it out, we'll cut the leg off."

"Yes," he cried, "can we do that? Yes, yes," he cried, relieved, thinking of it again. "Yes, we'll cut off my leg. My ankle, my ankle. Bring the ax. If you can't do it, call Hercules to cut off my leg. Now. Do it now."

"Stop it," she said, "and pay attention. That's only if it doesn't work. Everything is going smoothly. It couldn't be a better birth. You're doing everything just right. Now push, I say. Your little baby is about to be born. It wants to come out—there's a large view now of its head. Please stop thinking of yourself for once and give a good push. Remember, you're giving birth."

"My *baby*?" he said, opening his eyes suddenly.

"Yes," she said. "It's time to push it out now. Give a hard push from your gut all the way down to your foot."

"My own little baby," he said weakly during the moment when the pain seemed to be nowhere at all. "Yes, I think I forgot what it was all about." Sweat poured off of him even while resting.

"Don't worry," she said. "That's not unusual, but now is the time to gather your thoughts. Your little baby wants to come out."

"Yes, yes," he said opening his eyes up wide and then shutting them tight with a grimace. And then for a time he howled like a dog until—with a cold compress on his forehead, and his back and shoulders sponged off—he merely cried. "Hera, Hera, it's happening much more often," he whined. His voice was more of a whimper. It was as if a yellow light had gone out across the sky, a sickly yellow whimpering light. "Why won't it stop?"

"It will dear, it will. It won't be long now. Can you push? Can you give a big push or two? It won't be more than a minute or two."

"A minute or two?"

"Let's give it a push now. I'll help push. Here I am. We'll see your little baby's face in just a moment. Are you pushing now? Take a deep breath."

He inhaled then with such force that the trees on all the mountains, for several miles down from the top, were lost in the tempest. Then he took both his enormous hands and strangled his own leg, milking down to the ankle. "Yes," she cried, "yes!" she cried, beating on his back. "You're doing it!" And she rushed around to stand at the foot of the bed, for there was the whole head like a dark grapefruit. The back of it, wet and bloody and dark, looked down from its perch, fully born from between the two largest toes on that side.

"Push!" she cried, and she leaned down under and looked at its face. "Its eyes are open!" she exclaimed. "Its little squinty eyes are open! They're purple and it sees!" She ran her fingers around on the inside of its mouth, pulling the mucus out. "Push now or give your baby up!"

He took such a deep breath and gave such a grunt—

"And here it comes!" she announced. And the thing burst

the sole of his foot in half as he screeched. The little wet thing came tumbling out into her arms, screaming, too; and their voices were exactly four octaves apart: the new little baby's the highest, then Hera, then Zeus roaring away with laughter and pain, two octaves apart each pair of them.

"Let me see it, let me see it," he yelled. "Baby baby baby," Zeus cooed. "My little prettiest one." And he laid the tiny red and squalling boy against his chest in the safe cradle of his fore-arm and palm while he sang a song about lightning and rain.

"Yes," Teiresias says.

"I will not," Odysseus pleads.

"Yes," he says.

"I will not."

They are face to face. "Or you will never get home! Take me with you."

"It would be a sacrilege. The Gods will destroy me and my men."

The Old One will not relent. "Take courage, Odysseus. Think of it happily like that. Would Circe send you here idly? Take me out of this land of death and—for me—not death. Straighten my life like a strip of new iron, the kind that sprang up with those seven hoodlums that undid Thebes."

Teiresias shouted, lifting up his hands. "This is my moment. If there be a God, raise me up so you can lay me down again." And then again he turned insistently to the living man in front of him. "You, Odysseus, you are the one sent by Circe to take me away. I know the road but cannot carry my own weight."

Odysseus slapped his palms against his forehead and rubbed both eyes. "But to bring back the one who told the great Oedi-pos of his foul deeds! It would be a travesty."

Teiresias straightened out his coarse robe, subdued for a moment, and stared off into the dimly flowered field. "Oedi-pos? I had forgotten that," he sighed.

Odysseus looked up from his hands, incredulous. He had begun to shake from anger now; his fear, for one moment, a thing of the past. "You have forgotten that? You who remember everything? You who are known the world over for having said those most miserable of words to Oedipos?" The strips of his beard bobbed between his arms like the iron gate of a fence.

Again the Old One sighed as if nothing at all of consequence had been said. He hunkered down to think a grievous moment of his lost friends and relatives, and then to stare at what should have been the healing loveliness of asphodel, the wafting ghostly visages dancing there. "Yes, forgotten," he said again. "Is that so surprising? There was so much of the same. I remember his life, his past and future, of course, and the reasons for telling him. But the moment of revealing it—no." He studied the nap of his robe, fingered it. "The moments before, those were truly sad. Afterward, as it unwound just as I had foreseen, as the reports came in each day, yes, it was rewarding in a sense."

"Rewarding!" the warrior cried out. "A great man devastated and you call it that?"

Teiresias did not look up. "The greatest fall ever known, poor man, his wife lost, his eyes gouged out by his own jealous hands, his children cursed and all the rest. I never was wrong, and yet no one ever listened to me without seeking proof. By then I knew that much about myself; I was always correct. One does learn one's own limitations, of course." Teiresias tipped his head up toward the irate one. "Tell me when I said an untruth and I will let you go this instant, with a map engraved on your wrist."

With that Odysseus grew foully red in the face. He began to tremble and his hands went entirely white at the hilt of his sword. "I will not take you with me, no matter who you are, no matter how revered in the world. I would lose everything!" Then Odysseus raised up his own muscled arms in anger. "I have fallen into the hands of one who would sap the power of fleets."

Teiresias studied his own palms. "Only those who sound the

false alarm can be spoken of as such." Again he spoke quietly. "Embrace death if you like. I have no pity on you. You are a grown man who lives like an evil child torturing small animals."

Odysseus cried out hysterically then, but from all of it Teiresias could discern no words. Finally Odysseus came to a halt. There was the seer, completely untouched by his plea. "I am leaving now," Odysseus said. "I am going alone."

The heap of fabric at his feet stared calmly off into the blazing yellow field that bore no sun. "What will you do with your sword and battle-ax here—" it said, "threaten the dead?"

The thin man sat on a slab of granite and sobbed into his own beard. "I can't go home with a dead man on my back."

"Take my hand and then, just when you pass through the gate, let me hold onto the edge of your shield, for one moment only. That will be the end of it, I promise you."

Odysseus's legs had begun to shake from the knees to the ground like two unsteady walking sticks. "Not the end of you. The beginning and the beginning of the Gods' retribution! You say nothing, you say nothing at all of that."

Only time and contemplation in much silence will tell you what they mean. Though, in the dark of the night, your sight was no more than two painted clay marbles in your head, Teiresias, you saw clearly the ship pulling into the harbor and with it the beast. How did it happen? What small reference to snakes and the bearers of arms can have precipitated such a thing? The news is no news. Kadmos had only to spread the word: a Skythian ambassador to the Nile regions has embarrassed Thebes. And the town is to be emptied like drink from a cup. Already women waft lonely with their small children, here, there, as if dropped from the wool-tree to be borne by wind from place to place. By nightfall the rites will have passed; by sunrise young men will have been roused from their beds to stand in pairs with their elders. Old men and young will dress exactly alike so they may be better known for their allegiance, better identified.

Though strong daylight pierces the windows of the hut, there is now for Teiresias no light; she is blind to it in a way she did not know even as a blinded man, will not know even in the Underworld. The windows and walls, even the petty furniture in the abandoned room where she lies giving birth, the exquisite village and its fleeing residents outside, the plains and snow-capped crests of mountains beyond, even the future compelling and anathema both, and the past, kings, queens, palaces, slaves and commoners, even terror are gone. For all the pain, she cannot see even her own hands where they grip her knees. Blindly she would try to reach inside herself, her arms around her belly's sides, grappling to pull them out. Inside the small, small hole there is only at the fingertip a soft, wet, downy mat of feathered hair.

She has seen the terrifying forms of her twins, two separate colts, everything she has been and seen, two of them inside her blue-veined belly, outlined beneath her pendulous breasts. But there is no one to hear, not human or God, she thinks. The house is a cup around her now, with two babies deep inside. Her friends, lost to battle somewhere, cannot answer her; nor Zeus, nor anyone. Or surely they would have come. Wouldn't they? she asked herself. Already she whimpered: Get them out, please. Please, please stop. Get them out of me. Get them out. Now her fear swings forward and backward, for already she is breaking in half, again, in birth rhythms, as if she were being beaten inside with a bludgeon and then severed with an ax. With each contortion comes the certain knowledge that death is not only possible but imminent. The long retrospective of our future lives begins with birth.

And where was Hera now? Teiresias, he/she, whatever she is, may lose her babies, one or both; she may not be able to do the right thing, or anything at all for herself, alone; it has already been going on so long now, the sweating actuality of it. Her belly is a cataclysmic ball; she beats on it. She weeps from head and womb while between her legs it burns, as if with thousands of campfires in one white-hot circle of suffering. She knows it in the jaw and the kicked and battered bowels, in the broken vessels in the back of her throat and brain and lids, in the roaring pain in the top of her head, her teeth are held so tightly together that some are shattering. *Yes, Zeus, they are actually shattering.* Eternity may grip her here, or in a moment the head of beauty may tear its way out in a surge of ripped flesh, water, urine, and blood. In a moment, she hopes, her body will fall behind suddenly, a husk, dead or alive she doesn't care, to a sound like the breaking of small bones. Finally, she hopes she will hear in the next moment from some world the first baby's scream. Even days and nights have passed with the sounds of exodus rushing past the doors and windows of Thebes. She is praying now for sudden death. She buries her head and heavy body under blankets and quilts, like a beaten dog, hoping, if it does not stop, to suffocate herself.

Lying on the mat, small, impertinent, writhing, hallucinating thing, looking down at herself lying inside a glorified horse of all things: an immense false horse, higher than any wall. How can the wooden creature have been made so real and on such a grand scale? How can the ride be so smooth, be such agony, the sound of warfare so close and yet so remote? Teiresias watches as if ferried by birds in and around herself, sees as if from above, as the horse towers gargantuan over the wall of what she knows, though she has never seen it, to be their sister city, a city of grace. Below, in full view, atop the high, craggy cliff that overlooks rock and sea, the city's battlements rise from the ground for what seems like thousands of feet. And there she can see it now, too: the remote, ravaged homes and woodlands in the nearby countryside, beams from shepherds' huts, from oak and olive trees torn trunk from root and crop, everything from which the horse in which she dreams an existence has been made. It would be good for a time to dream of something else, to sleep.

But the carved city gates swing wide open like her knees, into the flowered countryside. The men have built the steed's expression to look exotic—as if it were a gift to Athena herself in their warriors' falsified retreat. Who could look upon its girth and teeth and nostrils, the saddle itself big as a house, its delicately painted eyes, without wonderment? Troy spills her citizens as if into a festival in a summer arcade—to welcome it. The very horse she rides captive within is presented to the city, as if in surrender, as if it were a gift to them. Of peace. And to the Gods, they say, the Gods who are said by men to will such things. Now behind the wooden bars of the animal's teeth, mouth within womb within mouth, Teiresias lies enmeshed in the vision of it. *Why can't you give these things up? What's the matter with you anyway? Try! for once! to live a normal life. Let time be.*

An odor rises now, *what is it?,* from the horse's bowels into the mouth where she lies, an odor of warriors' stench, of piss and sweat from all the men's anxious waiting hours, of the nauseous eruptions of the younger boys, nearly babies themselves, frightened and hidden in the hold with their weapons, nearly toys to them. Right now they might rather be at home with their mothers, or playing marbles in the streets. The scent rises up into the planked cavity, gullet, lips, and thickly beamed tongue, which have become for Teiresias the bedrock of a terrible predictive certainty. It is only his/her own life she cannot foresee. Then a terrified screaming rushes past the windows and doors. Is it Troy she hears, or Thebes? And the Trojan mount's eyes go wild at the vision of its own extraordinary vomiting: as its own tremendous maw disgorges its feverish, hidden warriors onto the supposed conciliatory scene in one of the greatest lies of all time.

Teiresias's small countrymen swarm like ants, Odysseus, too, importantly, not in peace as they have said, but in something quite otherwise. Odysseus and his friends stride in hordes, with piercing razors in their hands, dancing about, triumphant, with their lower bellies and upright genitals exposed. All too clearly Teiresias can see. On the paved streets of Troy below, women like herself in masses are being felled. Women like she is now, pregnant, and women like those she has been and known, women like her mother and grandmothers and Leiriope, even the youngest girls, awkward and beautiful and as shy before strangers as her friends Echo and Semele and Antiope, women like herself, these women are being stripped of all their clothes, with blades held to their throats, and forced to lie, shivering and terrified, opened before crowds, before a grappling penetration and then a mutilation with crude instruments. Women are crying with the shrieks of vanquished birds while even their littlest children drag bravely upon these men's bare and unrelenting knees.

But they have forgotten, these her countrymen, who they are and what they have loved and been, and for what their bodies have been made. Now, before her, they are less than even the lowest of animals, taking up children for sport. Ravaged women weep and plead for their children's release. Nakedness and rape, their own mutilation is nothing to them now as their children's small rounded limbs and faultless crying faces, their diminutive hands clutching air, are made to plummet in thousands from the city walls onto the horrified rocks below.

At first a silence came over her, and then a voice of rage, and then a silence again, broken only by the inescapable clashing of metal and breakable screaming living things. Teiresias rocks back and forth, howling as if she had lost her mind, to see these men disemboweling other nervous, fighting men, who have been forced into a battle within full sight of their own children, babies falling like a rain of pomegranates near their feet. Teiresias lies on a blanket and bawls like a child. These are the people of the present and the near future; they are not the people of dreams. And for Teiresias it is of no use to press her fists into the lids of her eyes, as she lies straddling the moment of her own babies, living or dead, in a town that is itself besieged, as she lies seeing the future like this. In this immutable moment, for every airborne little child's cry, even through her hands clogging up her ears, Teiresias can hear Echo's poignant song, in high-fluted children's calls, from cliff to cliff, the only rational voice in the multiple catastrophe. *Ma—ma—ma—ma—ma—ma* resounds again and again and again.

Finally, in the dreamed future of her life, he/she sees herself go, a tiny person oddly dressed with certain gifts of foresight that have never been much in dispute, to speak with the town's counselors, pleading for a revolution of thought, accompanied by a handful of women and men; finally he/she will go to speak with Zeus, only to be laughed at for her eccentricities. Teiresias labors in the knowledge, a knowledge she cannot accept. She cannot accept that the sorrows of war must be seen by even one parent, old or young, burning in any child's hair.

But now it comes. It is so quick now: first the rupturing, then the head and shoulder, arms and thighs, slippery eel, of one human child, and then the next. Two purple figures in the mire between her legs have yet to move. She runs her fingers inside their elastic mouths, she presses hard upon their backs. She turns them upside down. Inventing and inventing ways to make them live. She is hunched over them. *I said, look at me!* They have yet to move their ductile limbs. *My babies. Take your breath.* She kneads their backs, more roughly now, one and then the other. She slaps their backs. I have carried you. I have been speaking to you for so long. *Live!* She wrings their two blue bellies together like two doughy hands. *Live! You have given everything to me. Look at me. See my face. It is radiant with love for you.* Her voice swings back and forth in agony.

Will she have to lean down now, lost forever between her own bloody legs, and cut the cords where they hang out of her pelvis on two blue veins? Two blue stones, senseless pendulum, on strings?

She has actually jounced them together now, dead dead would-be living things she has carried inside of her, speaking to them. For months. Years it seems. For the first time in her life, she will not care for anything. She can barely see them through the rainfall that has come through the bashed window upon her face. She has shaken them in front of her: two dead sprawling frogs.

Before Teiresias's dazed eyes, the city burned, the holdings in the library, the paintings, music halls and schools, as though architecture and medicine and discovery meant not one thing. And after what Teiresias had seen happening to the women and children, to the youngest boys, to beautiful, vital, grown and old men, slashed and maimed—perhaps for a time Teiresias herself did not care much for anything, not now, not for anything she had loved. Not even for architecture or beauty, nor for the music played, so intricately, upon both the living and lost plazas and along the thoroughfares.

Names and images of streets and villages she had never seen came to her in languages she did not understand. White columns sprouted into buildings so tall she could not see the tops of them, and the sky was blotted out by flying things. The landscape rolled into burning rice paddies, into trampled cornfields and vines, into inflamed mountains and mounds of fluorescent dirt and concrete. And everywhere among her own, she could hear the piercing outcry of localities much like Troy: the cries of Alexandria and Thebes, of Mykenos, of Sarajevo, Saigon and Kuwait, Hiroshima, Guernica, Paris, Phnom Penh, of Boston, Treblinka and Wounded Knee, of a square called Tiananmen, and then, too, Atlanta, London and Iraq, Cape Town, Moscow, El Salvador, and New York.

She was made to watch the desolate women bound as slaves and herded into Grecian ships, and then at the end of the journey to be grafted into the stratum of a foreign land.

Certainly these beaten women—their children, lovers, parents, babies lost—would not care about anything for a time, she knew, not whether they washed up another woman's floors and dinner plates, nor whether they ate. And then finally it would come, she hoped, an upsurgence in their name. An upsurgence cunning and strong, indefatigable in its honed nonviolence.

The sound of it is sickening. When she rubs them together, their wet skins squeak. *Zeus!* She holds them against her, rocking, singing, *Look at me! Give me a chance. No matter what happens to us . . . I will always be your Mama now.* Two dead babies in a mutilated town. *To live in the present is intense. Learn. Living or dead, I'm your Mama now.*

In the hut surrounded by the pandemonium outside, the grinding of wheels and weaponry, the padding of anonymous feet, the muffled uncertainty, she holds her only children to her face. *No matter what happens, living or dead, I'm your Mama now.* But there! out from their little shriveled aqua mouths: two corks of yellow phlegm in golden would-be coins, a pair of ornaments for someone dead, or one released. They stick to her skin, two mucoid gifts. Wind fills the room. And rain. Down her face it pours. Their skin is fully flushed, a living pink. *Let me just look at you!*

They see me! she thinks. *Both of them.* She takes in their sweet breath and thinks no one will ever breathe such winds as these. *I am seen. In whatever way they see.* Teiresias puts their terrible rough sucking mouths to her breasts. There has never been such exquisite pain as when the milk comes pouring out. All her life she will live in this moment now. Their wet feathered heads bob up and down, twisting back and forth, losing her and finding her again. *Sing me your heart-torn cries. Such tears of joy.*

And just as surely as this part is over now and the next begins, there are two of them with her here in her own town, whatever is going on there, whatever will happen to them, these are her own children now. She gives them names: Historis with her puckered face gazing infinitely into the past, and then the second grasping one, one called Little Manto, seer.

How far will these daughters and their own sons and daughters see?

But already Teiresias is worrying as she gathers her robes around the three of them and bundles them against the deafening sound of warfare approaching oh so rapidly: if there had been any justice these two lives of all lives would have been one, even if they had had to be bound for life, past and present, like freaks at the shoulder and the hip. For surely, Teiresias believes, holding their bare, innocent, and living bodies inside her clothes and trying to stand, surely those who see the future should see the past, and the other way around, those who see another sex, color, creed should consider it in themselves. Teiresias knows as she looks at them, profoundly stirred in the grace of their one moment before they too must flee, that these her children are descended from everything she has been and seen: part everything, all colors, races, all benevolent creeds. She knows this one most simple and obvious of all things: though it is no less bloody or terrifying, it is a greater thing to give a life than to take it away.

And if the seer could have seen herself, as she was in actuality, set there on the rounded edge of the earthen world, she would have noticed a tiny woman, neither young nor old, still heavy as if with child, bearing two babies tightly in her arms, as best she could, running along the west road out of town. She would have noticed, too, that from between her own small feet and out from under her skirts she left the spoors of her blood and those of a world that went before. And in that blood, by way of two as-yet-attached cords, as if with the double-edged blade of an early plow, she raked two deep channels running infinitely parallel, through a seemingly boundless earth.

Teiresias was a silhouette in a dark scene, from the hem of his robe to the hood of his peaked cape. Teiresias shrugged while Odysseus eyed the shades once again drifting toward them. "There is nothing to say, Odysseus. The Gods are the Gods, there is no predicting. Perhaps it is their will. To resurrect a wise one, that is not an insignificant task. You will go down in history as a great one, not a bumbling idiot who desecrated innocent peoples on a lark and lost his loyal men to one fateful howl each. Yes, that might well be a sort of rebirth."

A shiver like a snake went visibly up the warrior's spine, curved around his neck under his beard, and crept into his eyes. "All right then. For my men."

"Always an honorable man. But let's be honest once: as always, this is for yourself. Now take my hand." He held it out, the thin white veil of a skin over twiglike veins underneath.

"But you have rotted away!"

A smile went over the old man's face. "Touch it or be it." And he threw back his hood in joyfulness, hobbling along, whistling to himself. "That is one thing I got right. Yes, indeed," he whispered to himself. "At least I waited till I died to rot. Now you yourself, my peripatetic friend, have been thoroughly rotted since your birth."

"What's that you said?" Odysseus asked, trudging along the riverbank, the dead man's hand held up gingerly like a feather in his one weaponless palm.

"Ah," Teiresias said, stopping to lean on his staff. "Look deeply there through the mist. You may glimpse it now. We have arranged a chorus for you, all those for whom you are responsible. There, too, is your mother; but for your absence she'd likely still be alive."

The great Odysseus turned then on the Knowing One, aghast. "Never has anyone said such a foul thing to me."

"Who would have dared?"

"Well, she, of course."

"She's never said a word against you from the start. Afraid of you, even when you were a child. Her thoughts went willy-nilly with fright when she saw the viciousness in you."

"I've had enough!" the man cried, trying to throw down the hand from his palm, but there it stuck as if it had grown out of his own skin like an elaborate wart, or a bird pecking at the inside of his hand. "What is it?" he cried. "Get off!"

"Be still," Teiresias whispered. "Be very still." At once the warrior ceased, thinking that his lack of commotion would release him from the Wise Man's grip. The glossy eyes looked straight at him. "You will be free of me when we pass into the other world." Odysseus opened his mouth to shout again, but something tapped his palm. "Be still now."

The greatly muscled man bit his lip, and his beard quavered with the anger in his voice. "I am trying to save my countrymen, and you are naming me, me, a common criminal. A common criminal. Circe said none of this."

"Even in the days before the bronze sword, Odysseus," the Wise Man said again in full voice, "even in the infinite history of Thebes as backward once it stretched, there were many like you—fortunately, few had enough rank. Hold off now, impetuous one. Gaze over there. Here they are: the ones you have slain and lost. If only I could show you so brilliantly the boys you are about to lose."

"Tell me now!" the warrior commanded, waving about the one hand Teiresias held, but it was as if a praying mantis had stuck itself to his palm. "Please tell me who it is."

In disbelief, Teiresias rubbed his other hand over the top of his nearly hairless head. "Have you already forgotten my terrible words? But," he sighed, "it is like you. Your forgetfulness begets atrocity. That is the nature of the world. So it will always be, you can rely on these things. Here now, a little more slowly, here is the nursery of your deeds. The babes bloodied at your hands. And here, your own babe." Pale faces of every age and color looked up at him.

"My own? My own? What became of it? Which is it? Why is it here?" he cast about frantically looking at face after face. "Why did I not know that we had another one? Perhaps after our ship had gone—" Odysseus swept his massive hand through his thick graying hair. "But my Penelope, how she must have grieved. I didn't know. Truly, I had no idea. What was it—a boy or girl?"

Teiresias put his head back and moaned. How tightly his skin had come to wrap his skull. What an effort to stretch the lips, to listen to Odysseus going on.

"Why do you laugh when you have caused me such pain?" the warrior cried. "What further wretchedness do you see? What else? What else is festering like that sore you call your mind?"

"It is only a trick for the sake of your audience," he said somberly. "It is my first falsehood. If I'd embraced your way, perhaps I'd have let you believe it still. No child of yours is yet here. Other than these that once belonged to your world."

The dead infants and children stared on, the boys and girls, the brides and their young loves, their mothers and fathers, the dignified older dead. For a moment a sound like the cacophony of alarmed birds went up among them. It seemed to sweep and turn around their heads. Together they were making a hissing sound through the clattering of their teeth. Then Teiresias cried it out again to the powers overhead, "Raise me up so you can lay me down again!" It was then that Odysseus put his own will to his decision. The Odysseus, horrified, yanked the Old Wise One from the banks of Lethe, swept him into the alarmed protection of his arms, and began to run. Toward home.

Up, up out of the ripe earth, called forth by a distant communion with the dead, Teiresias comes plowing earth, gasping just as his ancestors did, with his worn and tattered head. On his arm, transplanted after all these years, is the blood-red mark: Theban Spear, Sign of Kadmos, Sign of Sown Men. Odysseus has long since been left to wend his own way home.

"Life!" Teiresias cries, wailing with joy in an ancient language no one can yet understand.

"Life, life, incomparable, fractious life!" Again and again he wails it as the world comes into view. Again alive, no less wise, Teiresias stands, buried to the chin, and stares as if from the nether lips of the modern world. All around him, summer light pours down through massive oaks. The ground is dappled everywhere. Two lambs and one dark heifer gaze at him over the stone wall. In the cove the little boats rock benignly against docks and shore. And from here to there, behind the barn and down the rose-hipped hill, the land is peopled by his dreams. Here a face, there those faces of men and women he has seen from another place and time. Myriad others drift over a long green lawn, while overhead, a circling of birds: then and now, here and there, as if his mother had described it to him. Across the road, in a white-painted, wooden structure, are brilliantly colored panes with portraits of Gods and mortals he had long ago foreseen.

Near him now, slender feet in sandals wander down the hilly slope. Small hoops of wire stand looped across the lawn. A little girl swings her mallet, and out from beside the long white slightly muddied dress, one of the wooden balls strolls. And here, too, the hairy ankles of a dog, black and white, up close, sniffing now, barking at the strange phenomenon: Teiresias reborn.

Teiresias cocks his head toward the music of their game: the clunking together of red and blue spheres, the exquisite oranges and greens. Then through thick blue-green summer grass, it comes: slightly up, slightly down over the slightly uneven ground, a bright red ball and the little girl quickly after it.

Now Teiresias can see it, too, reflected in the turning side of the ball, his old dream renewed. There it is, too, rebounded at the centers of the little child's eyes: scarves flutter as two women deliberate their near-escape. In the bright red car they fly along a stone-gray road, pulling past a vehicle Teiresias could never before identify. A tarp lifts up, carried by a rising wind. The women can see it now: the long cylindrical object where it rides on the back of the truck. The women pull past it, their harmless vehicle in front of the metallic cone.

Now Teiresias can see it repeatedly, the overlay of time like lacquers on the surface of a fine table, like a painting in pentimento, or in a representation of the world he once knew on the glossy side of an urn. There beneath the missile, in a life now turned to memory and endless dust, just as his mother once pointed out to Ameinius on the side of a vase: a hippopotamus stands in obsolete waters staring at a man. Teiresias can see it, too: paint cracking at the side of the urn as a pink sweat rises on the thick hide of the beast. Small ears pivot like lilies on their stalks. What can be heard through the ears of this animal? Gen-